OBAMASAURUS

The Legend of How
the Judeo-Christian Dinosaur Nation
Was Depopulated and
Suffered Extinction

Is Depopulation Possible Today?

....

**The Redistribution
of Wealth and Population Control
Political Satire
for**
Young and Mature

ROSE M COLOMBO

INK START MEDIA
5710 W Gate City Blvd Ste K #284
Greensboro, NC 27407

CONTENTS

DEDICATION

A Keepsake of How Evil Works While Good People Sleep
The New Millennium

This book is dedicated to all my brothers and sisters around the world who have suffered at the hands of tyrannical leaders; unjust laws, discrimination, hate crimes, excessive punishments or excessive taxation. It is when we do not peacefully unite and resist against the evil that bad things happen to good people such as genocide, depopulation and extinction. May you be blessed with new leaders who will restore your nations and your lives and help bring peace and love and harmony into the world.

INTRODUCTION

The stranger peaked Noah's curiosity. Noah stared at the old sage and asked, "What bad things will happen if I fail on this mission?" The stranger said, "I can't reveal the bad curse that will come upon the world because they turned their backs on their Judeo-Christian God and his universal Ten Commandments."

CHAPTER 1

Summer of 2008

The summer of 2008 wasn't any different than in the past, except that it radiated unprecedented temperatures and a blistering heat wave across the nation. There was a definite and noticeable climate change. It was a long hot summer for Noah, a man who didn't complain much, but he couldn't recall such a hot summer. He kept a handkerchief with him so he could wipe away the sweat that dripped down his brow from time to time. He enjoyed relaxing inside of his modest four-bedroom home which he inherited from his dad. Noah believed that his dad died without fulfilling his dream and Noah had a burning desire to fulfil his real father's lifetime dream.

The sizzling hot summer nights didn't cool down until midnight, so Noah and his neighbors usually sat outside on their large front porches until the temperatures cooled down. They slept with their bedroom windows open allowing the warm summer breeze to blow through an open pathway and flow into the rooms and circulate. As Noah sat on the front porch, he looked around and was pleased that the neighbors kept the middle class neighborhood groomed with willow trees shaded along the sidewalk. He felt safe.

But one night after Noah fell into a deep sleep, he felt a soft cool breeze brush against his face until it awakened him from a pleasant dream. He was irritated that his unusual dream had been interrupted. Noah was considered an introvert and somewhat of a home body, but his students and colleagues respected him as a distinguished and knowledgeable archaeologist. He chose his esoteric group of friends wisely. His close friends referred to him as a wild stallion, who didn't like to be corralled, but it didn't bother Noah. He enjoyed his freedom. His mixture of Red Neck and conservative friends teased him because he dated many pretty women, but he never asked any of them to marry him. His friends would laugh and jokingly say, "Noah, you're like the runaway groom, instead of the runaway bride." Although, Noah liked the ladies, he grew accustom to being single and never quite felt the same passion for the ladies as he had for his profession. He tossed and turned while trying to get comfortable, but he couldn't fall asleep immediately as his mind wouldn't rest.

Sometimes, Noah would jump out of bed to grab a late-night snack from the fridge, but on this one night, he felt too lazy and restless to make a snack. He thought about settling down and having a family, but then he'd rationalize that taking on the responsibilities of a wife and children would interfere with his lifelong dream of traveling to faraway lands. He felt he had to find his purpose in life, so he wouldn't regret marrying and being tied down.

Suddenly, his job popped into his head and he thought I'm so lucky. I work at a job that I love. His mind wandered even more and he mumbled, "I really do enjoy teaching young people at the university and watching their excitement whenever I discuss my adventures in faraway lands. It is an amazing feeling." Noah's passion to learn about the herbivorous dinosaurs that roamed the earth made him feel alive. He never tired of his research and tried to figure out the true facts of how the magnificent dinosaurs known for their excessive longevity were depopulated and wiped off the face of the earth.

The warm summer breeze continued to blow into his bedroom and caused him to open his sleepy eyes, but he continued to toss and turn. He couldn't sleep, so he stacked his fluffy pillows against the solid mahogany headboard and sat up. He leaned back against the pillows and rubbed his tired eyes. A few minutes later, he slowly swung his long legs around the side of the bed and sat there for a minute while he shoved his oversized feet into a pair of soft beige slippers made of cozy suede and soft leather.

After a few minutes of standing on his feet, he felt somewhat dizzy, so he slowly stood up straight and raised his muscular arms above his head and stretched his long body. He breathed deeply and felt invigorated. He didn't understand why he felt so energized and anxious to get up out of bed. He looked at the clock and said, "Good grief, it can't be 1:00 in the morning." Noah's thoughts wandered back to his dream. His intriguing dream felt so real. He laid in bed thinking about his dream. He recalled seeing a shadow of an old man who told him to prepare for a very long journey. He remembered that the voice was soft, but firm. The shadow appeared to be a man whose face he couldn't see but whose voice he could hear. He remembered that the voice informed him that he would discover a rare treasure that would be invaluable. He felt bothered and fascinated by his dream, but he wasn't quite sure why and dismissed it as a figment of his imagination.

Noah felt disoriented after he awakened from his sleep and decided to walk into his walk-in closet where he grabbed a suitcase and set it on top of his bed. He didn't really know why he grabbed the suitcase, but he checked it out to make sure it was in good condition. He stopped for a moment and mumbled, "What am I doing?" He looked around the room and felt confused.

He walked over to a mahogany antique desk handed down from his grandfather and sat down. He reached for the switch and turned on the Tiffany lamp attached to a dark metal stand. He cherished that particular lamp because it belonged to his mother. He truly missed her very much. Unfortunately, she died of pneumonia, when he was a young man, which left him and his dad devastated. Noah believed that his dad missed his mom so much after her death that his dad eventually died of a broken heart. Noah didn't have any brothers or sisters, so his career was the love of his life after he lost both parents.

Noah slowly leaned over and looked at the large globe setting on a wooden stand next to his desk and began running his thick fingers across the globe. He didn't understand why he was searching for a destination or why he packed a suitcase, but he felt a sudden desire to travel. Even as a child, he believed that he had a mission in life. His feelings were rarely wrong. Noah's father taught him to follow his instincts so he could make good decisions throughout his life.

The thought of flying across the ocean and exploring an isolated area of the world intrigued him. He felt excited just thinking about it. He dreamed of exploring a remote land and searching for artifacts. Noah's interest with the dinosaur world began when he was a small child. He reminisced about his childhood as he sat in his thick brown leather chair and remembered his favorite toy, a large dinosaur, which his father gave to him on his seventh birthday. The dinosaur was special because it stood tall. Noah would push a button and the dinosaur's eyes lit up. The dinosaur stomped across the floor and roared. Noah pretended that his dinosaurs were his friends, but only when his best friends weren't around.

The old wooden toy box in Noah's bedroom was stacked high with dinosaur toys. Each dinosaur had a special name. But, the one dinosaur that his father purchased for Noah on his seventh birthday was his favorite dinosaur. Noah named his special dinosaur, Obamasaurus, and he pretended that Obamasaurus was fearless and bold. Even as a child, Noah pretended that he lived during the age of the dinosaurs. He would use his wild imagination and pretend that he lived in the jungles near a majestic mountain and imagined himself riding on the backs of the dinosaurs as well as climbing in the trees. Consequently, Noah chose a career which provided him the opportunity to explore his dream involving the dinosaur world. Noah was very familiar with the dinosaur world as an adult. In fact, his peers recognized him as a prominent archaeologist and respected professor at the university.

Noah worked at the local university and took his work seriously but his close friends weren't college professors. His special friends were guys that he'd grown up with in his neighborhood. In fact, after work, they'd meet every night at a local pub for about an hour sipping on a beer and munching on peanuts. He teased his friends and referred to them as Red Necks because they supported strict constitutionalists for public office. His friends were adamant about defending the right to bear arms. His best friends included Mitt, Paul, Issa, Sean, and Joe. Mitt and Paul were businessmen and Sean worked in media. Joe spent his career in law enforcement and happened to be the local Sheriff. He also admired another dear friend, Clinton, who informed the group that he was a libertarian, but Noah considered himself a conservative and a Liberal all rolled into one.

One night, Noah left his friends at the local pub and stopped for a quick dinner at the Horseshoe Café. He liked the old landmark restaurant with home style cooking. Afterwards, he walked home alone. He couldn't stop thinking about the dream that awakened him the night before and his desire to travel intensified. After he arrived home, he made a cup of hot tea and grabbed a book from the bookshelf. He enjoyed laying on the couch in the living room to read. He picked up an old book that his friend had given to him, but he shelved. The stories in the book about injustices shocked him. He believed that most people didn't have a clue what was happening in the government.

"I can't believe how the world has gotten so corrupt," Noah said. Actually, he felt guilty for not being more involved in the nation's political issues, especially when the scandals were so very intense. Noah couldn't put the book down, but he looked up at the clock, and it was getting very late, so he thought, it's time to get to bed. He pulled himself up off the couch and put the book down on the desk and walked to the bedroom and jumped on his bed and got into a fetal position and fell asleep. The night quickly turned into morning. The alarm clock went off. Noah awakened from his deep sleep. He felt good when he woke up and crawled out of bed. He headed for the kitchen so he could switch on the coffee pot.

As a creature of habit, Noah made a pot of coffee at night before going to bed. He just wanted to plug it into the wall when he got up. He liked the thought that the coffee was perking while he was getting ready for work. He headed for the bathroom to wash up and then grabbed a pair of slacks and a shirt and tie and after he got dressed, he looked at himself in the mirror and said, "Not too shabby." Noah sauntered into the kitchen and the coffee flavor peaked his taste buds. He opened the cupboard to grab his favorite coffee mug. He slowly poured hot coffee into the cup as he enjoyed the aroma in the room. He picked up the spoon on the counter in the sugar bowl and he always added 4 teaspoons of sugar and easy on the creamer. Noah took a sip of the steaming hot coffee and breathed in. He said, "Wow, perfect."

A thump hit the back door and it was the morning newspaper. He immediately walked over to the door and opened it. He leaned down and grabbed the newspaper from the ground and walked back into the kitchen and sat down at the kitchen table with his coffee. Noah read the entire newspaper before going to work. After a few sips of coffee and reading the news and the economic status of the nation, he sighed. He noted that more people were filing bankruptcy and their homes had gone into foreclosure because they had signed onto the government's creative financing, but, sadly, the buyers discovered that they couldn't afford the house payments and taxes. He sighed when he looked at the date on the newspaper and mumbled, "Oh yes, this is the day after the presidential election, November 4, 2008.

Noah looked at the photo of the newly elected president and he thought, well, he has a great smile, but for some reason, his eyes aren't trustworthy. And, he appears somewhat arrogant, but I could be wrong. Noah mumbled, "How did an unknown and unidentified stranger get elected by a majority of Americans to the highest office in the land without identifying himself?" Noah recalled watching the news on television and prior to the elections, he couldn't believe that millions of Americans were actually chanting, "Yes he can." He remembered thinking that the American people must have bought the snake oil because they never asked, "Yes, he can do what?" They were following a stranger in the night, he thought.

Of course, Noah was confused why Americans would vote for an unidentified stranger, but he thought, it must be that he's likeable and charismatic or somewhat of a novelty, after all, he is a Mulatto, which was unprecedented. Noah never believed in his heart that the new president was completely honest. The newly elected U.S. President remained a mystery to the majority of citizens as the people knew very little about him. Noah wasn't pleased with the country's globalist agendas, which included outsourcing U.S. jobs and technology to anti-American nations, or trampling on the Constitution of the United States, even though he tried to avoid political discussions, but he couldn't help but feel disturbed by what he was hearing on the news and reading in the newspaper.

Noah thought, we think if we don't talk about politics, and we stay out of politics that we'll escape the controversy, but all laws rendered affect everyone's life. He said, "I guess, we've forgotten that the American people are the government and placed too much trust in the hands of politicians, so now we'll see what happens." Noah talked to himself a lot. After all, he lived alone in the house and talking out loud about the issues helped him find answers.

Nonetheless, Noah's work involved research, so he decided to research the new president's background. He couldn't explain why he felt a need to research his background because he never felt compelled in the past to research any president's background. Noah was concerned that the new president hadn't produced a certified copy of his U.S. Birth Certificate as required by Article II, Section 1, Clause 5, of the U.S. Constitution, which is the Rule of Law. He also learned through his research that the unidentified U.S. President had ties to radical and communist mentors and his family members belonged to anti-American radical communist organizations, which was quite stunning. The mainstream media reported only the fluff not the fact that the written goal of radicals was to wipe out America.

It was difficult for Noah to find any articles that disclosed any information of significance relating to the new president and this bothered him a lot. Noah felt that radical leaders from around the world could now pose a threat to Western Civilization and attempt to impose their laws on Americans or even attempt to deny freedom to Americans if his mission and his sympathies lied elsewhere, but with so little truth in the news, there wasn't much to go on. He recalled that the former President of the USA embraced Communist China and globalism and he felt that was a big mistake.

Noah attempted to reveal his research and information with his friends, but he quickly learned that most Americans and even his strong constitutional Red Neck friends and Libertarians or conservatives alike sometimes didn't want to listen to some of his information. They discredited his information as conspiracy theories. Noah gave up attempting to prove his theories on his views or show evidence to anyone who appeared to be a blinded zombie and didn't bother to research the United Nation's Agenda 21 or The Patriot act, Lock Step or the NDAA

Law. Noah was concerned about the excessive radiation that was being used on Americans. He was concerned because Hitler used radiation and experimental injections during WW II on the Jews and millions of people he referred to as non-humans. In fact, Hitler killed more than 200,000 kids with experimental and trial injections and made others sterile, paralyzed or caused heart inflammation.

Noah was aware of the direct adverse health effects of radiation which can cause adverse reactions, which can't be reversed once radiated, such as cataracts, sterility, aging, cancer and death. He was concerned about the microchips that have been manufactured and the push to insert a chip in the brain or under the skin on the hand or forehead as if we're no more than government property, chattel, slaves being forced into servitude against our will by placing fear in the minds of the general public. He was concerned about the implementation of Agenda 21 and the written and stated strategic goal of reducing the world's population by 90% by the year 2050. He read the wealthy members of secret societies appear to be seeking agendas to save the planet by reducing the population of God's creations in order to Redistribute the Wealth of the World to the wealthy 10% who plan on surviving.

Noah warned his friends about the mandated nationalized healthcare, which includes death panels through the implementation of rationing and denying health care treatments to Americans but not for illegals or alleged refugees who were exempt from signing up or paying up or being punished with jail and fines. He warned his friends that the new health care laws included the implementation of death panels. Euthanasia. Early-end-of-life counseling. Taxpayer funded abortions and experimental vaccines worldwide. Where was this country's moral compass?

CHAPTER 2

The Encounter

Although, Noah felt alone when it came to his political views, his excitement about his dream and his desire to carry out a mission across the oceans on a faraway land was his focus. He felt that he did his best to warn Americans about his thoughts about the new President, but he felt that he had to move on. The truth was that Noah didn't want the administrators of the University to discredit his research when he submitted his application because of political views. He tried not to discuss politics with the students or with his colleagues.

Noah was a positive thinker and felt that his request for a grant to travel and search for artifacts and clues about the lost dinosaur world would have a better chance of being approved if he focused on his career and his students. He decided to begin writing his proposal after class ended and study various places in the world that may have the clues that he needs before going on such an adventure. He needed to find the right words about his purpose and his mission as well as the worth and value to the university and the students and mankind.

Approximately, one month later, Noah was sitting at his desk in his office at the university eating his lunch. He was reading an article when he heard a slight noise. Creak. Creak. Creak. He looked at the door and he noticed the door opened slightly. His eyes looked up and he felt a strange presence as if he wasn't alone, but he didn't see anyone. He kept reading the article. Noah felt as if someone was in the office with him. He looked up and he thought his eyes and his mind were playing tricks on him. He kept staring. He was confused. He felt as if he was staring at a mystical male figure standing before him. Noah's mind was spinning as his eyes opened wide with surprise. A frail, slender elderly man appeared out of nowhere. He stood about 5'9" tall and he remained silent. He was wearing a beautiful red silk kimono with gold embroidery. He stood silent.

Noah felt as if the man appeared out of thin air. He asked, "Do you have an appointment with me?

The elderly man chuckled and replied, "No, Noah, I don't make appointments, but you have an appointment with me and with destiny." The stranger with the curious pale face wearing the long red silk kimono tied a gold sash around his waist that was adorned with rare sparkling diamonds and precious stones.

The Elder carried a long stick crafted from Mother of Pearl. It was beautifully carved with strange writings and symbols. Noah thought that his eyes must be deceiving him.

"Surely, I'm not speaking to a wise old sage from the past," he muttered. Maybe, it's something that I've eaten. Noah was fascinated. He began to feel somewhat comfortable. Curiosity was taking over as he became more intrigued. Suddenly, the mysterious old sage lifted the Mother of Pearl stick above the desk. A flash of light struck like a lightning bolt. The lightning bolt startled Noah. The globe sitting on Noah's desk began to spin around and around.

Noah was surprised. He said, "How did you do that?

The sage appeared peaceful and yet, magical and mysterious. The long white beard and white thinning hair flowing on the stranger's head and face resembled thick locks of white cotton. His eyes twinkled with a soft caramel color as he stared into Noah's eyes as if he was hypnotizing him. Noah felt connected to the sage. There was a colorful aura of rainbow colors surrounding the elderly sage who demanded Noah's full attention.

Noah relaxed. He began to feel as if he'd known the old sage for many years, but how could that be he thought. That's not possible. He hoped that the wise old sage would stay awhile. Noah wanted to know more about him. Noah asked, "Won't you sit down, sir?"

The frail elderly man smiled. He emitted an aura of gentleness and grace.

The sage responded, "No thank you. I know you would like me to stay and visit with you, but my time is limited and valuable and I am on a mission. There are many things that I must explain to you and I don't have much time. I must return and report to my Masters.'

The elderly sage was polite but spoke in a firm tone of voice. He said, "As I've stated. My time here is brief. You must listen carefully, Noah. I shall not repeat what I am about to reveal to you."

Noah's curiosity peaked and he was intrigued. Noah asked, "May I ask your name?"

The wise old sage said, "My name is not important." He said, "I have many names and many faces. You may call me, Dr. Lee."

Noah nodded his head and said, "Okay, Dr. Lee. I shall refer to you as you wish."

A moment of silence passed. One could hear a pin drop in the room. The office door slammed. The door shut closed and startled Noah.

The wise old sage stated, "Don't be afraid, I'm not here to harm you, but help you." Noah stared into his twinkling crystal eyes. The wise old sage stated, "Listen to me carefully, Noah. You have been chosen by higher beings. These wise men prefer to remain anonymous. They are powerful beings and I am not permitted to reveal their names, so please don't bother to inquire. These wise men of the universe have determined that you are a trustworthy man. They voted and you were chosen to complete a very special mission."

Noah was fascinated and speechless. The mysterious sage stated, "I know everything about you. For example, you've been restless and you don't know why. You've applied for a leave of absence because you yearn to travel to distant and remote lands and venture out into the world that came before your world. Your request shall be approved." Noah looked surprised and puzzled.

The sage stated, "It's of the utmost importance for you to travel to a faraway land that lies across the oceans. Once you arrive at your destination, which shall be revealed to you, you must do as you are instructed without fail. If you succeed, you alone will hold the secret that may save humanity from extinction."

Noah felt confused, but he was excited about the expedition. The old wise sage raised his precious stick again and the globe sitting on Noah's desk began spinning around and around. Suddenly the globe stopped. The sage pointed to a specific place on the globe with his stick. He said, "This is your destination where you shall begin your mission." He then reminded Noah not to reveal the mission to a living soul which isn't dishonest because he was going to a secret place in search of ancient artifacts related to the world of the dinosaurs.

He looked directly at Noah and said, "This mission must be kept in strict confidence. I can't stress this enough. You must never reveal your mission to anyone. Do not tell anyone about me for they will not believe you and they'll mock you. If you do tell anyone, your days will be cursed," he warned. Noah once again promised not to breathe a word to anyone about the sage or the confidential mission.

The elegant elderly sage remarked, "You will travel to a hidden land which was once known as the last Judeo-Christian Dinosaur Nation. This is where you must search for the lost dinosaur tablets etched in stone that holds the secret to saving mankind. Humanity is being set up for extinction."

Noah felt excited but uncertain at the same time. The elder stated, "Noah, you must find the secret to saving your own species as there are tribes who have been made extinct since time began by other tribes who wiped them out."

Noah was speechless. The gracious wise sage said, "You must search for the secret dinosaur legend carved into stone on the dinosaur Tablets hidden inside of the lost and forgotten cave that was built on the side of a majestic mountain top where the dinosaurs once roamed. I cannot reveal the exact location on the mountain where the dinosaur Tablets remain hidden or else the legend will be destroyed and lost forever. It is the destiny of the chosen one, which is you, to locate the ancient hidden dinosaur Tablets. I can tell you that the dinosaurs once ruled the planet and were feared by all."

Noah said, "But what if I fail?"

You shall not fail. You are not one to give up on a mission so important to mankind. I can tell you that the Judeo-Christian dinosaurs were intelligent.

They could communicate or else they couldn't survive. The message began in 2008 B.C. and there are important dates for this time in history which are 2008, 2009, 20011 2012, 2019, 2020, 2021, 2025, 2027, 2030, and 2050. There are certain historic events that may or may not have occurred or will occur in each of those years.

Noah recalled pastors telling stories in the past of how the evil ones are shaping the events of what will occur or won't happen in the future after the year 2000. They said that there will be major events that will determine whether God's children will survive or succumb to a worldwide genocide when evil men and women attempt to bring about the end times. The challenge is if God's children, good men and women, stay the course and resist evil so they can usher in the world of peace and the Great Awakening of Jubilation. The pastors warned that we are in a spiritual battle of evil versus good that will happen upon the earth.

As you know, Noah, many bad things have already occurred since the New Millennium, but mankind is stubborn and refuses to listen to moral people.

The American people are brainwashed by the glitz, explicit sex, drugs and violence seen on television produced by the evil ones. I'm sure you've noticed that your planet is experiencing unprecedented storms since the year 2000 which mankind refers to as "global warming or "climate change during the "New Millennium. Humanity is at a crossroads and there is little time left.

Noah thought about the news and all the fear mongering. Housing Crisis. Bankruptcies. Inflation. Warnings of coming events. Y2K2. 9/11. Mayan end times on 12-12-12. Threats of WW III. China, Russia and Iran coming together against the USA. Lone shooters appear to be drugged out. The unprecedented storms and floods continue to increase since Katrina. The attack on the OKC. Planes disappearing. Ships disappearing. Kids disappearing. Anthrax scares. News reporting on unprecedented storms occurring around the world. Raging wildfires. Hurricanes. Tornadoes. Floods. Volcanoes. Tsunamis. Earthquakes. Wars. Radiation. Nukes. Chemical Warfare. Worldwide Abortions. Increased Suicides and Homelessness. Increased Viruses and Diseases. Increases in Divorce. Illegal drugs. It appears that genocide versus survival is on a collision course. Somehow humanity continues to survive but only if they remain in God's army.

The stranger peaked Noah's curiosity. He stared at the old sage and asked, "What bad things will happen if I fail on this mission?"

The wise old stranger said, "I can't reveal the bad curse that will come upon the world because so many have turned their backs on their Judeo-Christian God and his universal Ten Commandments. The Dinosaurs realized that the time would come when other species would be forced to protect themselves from evil reptilian beings who will appear charismatic, but they shall come to deceive, cheat, kill steal, and destroy the Judeo-Christian Nations worldwide by reducing the population of the planet. The rumor is that they are among us and they are shape shifters.

"I can tell you that God wasn't pleased with the Judeo-Christian Dinosaur Nation or the anti-Judeo-Christian dinosaur nations for years. The American people have become "tolerant" of evil crimes against humanity. Men and women's hearts have become hardened and complicit as they call abortions legal and that it's a woman's right to end the life of her baby on Judeo-Christian soil, which is a depopulation program, enacted by anti-God and anti-Judeo-Christians. The evil ones will mandate experimental drugs and injections or surgeries upon humanity. Scientists have been buying baby's organs, DNA, blood human tissue and aborted fetal tissue. They call it Science, but they have blood on their hands. Humanity has excused the increased number of pedophiles attempting to legalize pedophilia for their instant self-gratification and justification of their crimes against children. God will not tolerate these sins forever," Dr. Lee stated.

He continued, "God warned men and women not to harm children.

Celebrities and Liberals protest their opposition against killing animals. Bugs. Turtles, Fish. Mammals. Bees. Environment. How is it that they don't care about 70,000,000 natural-born babies wiped out by abortion. Babies are needed to preserve the future of the world or there won't be a future for America. Why aren't babies on their priority list of endangered species?"

Noah recognized the anger and sadness in the elder's eyes.

Noah pondered if the Americans and Europeans are a foolish species. We punish people for killing a man who harms or kills a pregnant woman, but we allow more babies to die on a seamless assembly line at Planned Parenthood tables before or after they take their first breath. We've killed more natural-born American babies than all troops who were killed by foreign enemies on the battlefields. How could that be? Depopulating natural-born babies will wipe out sovereign nations because sovereign nations need natural-born babies to grow up and continue preserving their sovereign nations, race, ethnicity, civilizations, culture, foods, music, laws, and way of life in the future. Without babies, there is no future for humanity and yet, there are Billionaires who want to end procreation and heterosexuality.

He felt that the government sends young people to fight and risk their lives or health on the battlefields so that the victorious government can control the oil or the land that they conquer or both. And the wealthy exploit the Third World nations and use their people for slave labor so they can make huge profits while they pay the slaves 25 cents per hour or $1 per day. How can we allow this to happen when we were founded on a Judeo-Christian foundation and U.S. laws were rooted from the Bible and the 10 Commandments? Where is our moral compass? He mumbled, "Is oil, minerals, gold, silver, diamonds, and pearls more valuable than human life?

Noah began to think more about what is the real end game of World Leaders and wealthy New World Order CEO's? How many Third World countries have been stripped of their commodities, trees, fruits, plants, Rain Forest, lumber and spices by Wall Street, not by us? How many times has the U.S. government and wealthy New World Order CEOs used the workers in Third World Nations for slave labor? The government screams employers should give Americans who flip hamburgers $15 per hour, but they are okay with Wall Street paying indigent foreign slave labor 25 cents per hour. Noah shook his head. And, public servants have no problem living off taxpayers for life despite the wealth that they've acquired mysteriously.

The sage spoke up, "Unfortunately, in today's world, mankind believes wealthy and famous people are gods. They dismiss wife beating, child abuse; rape, murder, and pedophilia as tolerable if the abuser is wealthy or has a title or fame and connections. This is why 20% up to 25% of all people thrown into jail are innocent because they haven't any money to hire high powered lawyers to defend them in a court of law, so they plead guilty and plea bargain out of fear to a crime they may not have committed which wipes out "due process of law" in some ways.

Noah zoned out and wondered why teachers and administrators of public schools were okay with teaching K-12th grade students that it's okay to play violent video games or watch violent cartoons or movies that sexualize kids. Glorify sex. Promote sex outside of marriage. Glorify abortion. Adultery. Illicit drugs. Alcoholism. Cigarettes. Pornography. Many of these immoral teachings are aired on television during family time. Dr. Lee realized that he caused Noah to think about the real issues of the day that he read about, but didn't oppose, so that made him part of the problem and not the solution.

The eloquent sage tapped his Mother of Pearl walking stick on the desk and startled Noah bringing him out of his deep thought. Dr. Lee remarked, "Noah, you have been chosen to help save humanity and to bring change that can help the masses get back on track. The evil ones must be purged from the Judeo-Christian Nation and be held accountable for their evil behaviors. If you fail to find the hidden and untouched secret dinosaur Tablets, then all of God's creation on the planet will self-destruct. Mankind will self-destruct and destroy all that God created. You know the old saying that it's when good people do nothing and allow their minds to be frozen with fear by the evil ones that bad things happen."

Noah's face appeared worried, but he remained silent. He looked at the wise old man and said, "Why would the anonymous group choose me?"

The wise and serious sage said, "Don't ask why, but do as you're instructed and don't breathe a word to anyone about this mission to a living soul. Do you understand?" Noah nodded.

Dr. Lee stated, "The lost and precious secret dinosaur Tablets were carved into stone and left behind by two male Elders. One of the Elders was the well-respected and moral Ruler of the Judeo-Christian Dinosaur Nation."

Noah asked, So should I think of this as a supernatural battle of good vs. evil?" The sage nodded and said, "yes." Noah looked satisfied with such a mission.

Noah wondered if mankind was entering into the end times upon the earth which was recorded in the Book of Revelations in the New Testament of the Bible. He wondered if the world leaders were conspiring to declare war and commence WW III that could lead to the battle of Armageddon. Noah looked down at his notes and asked the mysterious sage if that was possible, but there wasn't an answer. He looked up from his desk and the elegant sage vanished. Noah felt sad because he had so many questions, but it was too late.

The clock on the desk was ticking loudly. It was 6:00 p.m. He sat at his desk for a minute and took a deep breath as he gathered his notes and grabbed his briefcase and carefully inserted his notes into his briefcase. "It has been a long day," he sighed. He decided to walk home and stop somewhere to get a bite to eat on the way." He got up from the chair, grabbed his jacket and leather case and headed out the door. Noah stared at the door for a moment remembering what he experienced and then he closed the door and headed home.

The thought of having his request to fund a sabbatical across the oceans appeared farfetched to Noah. He dismissed the thought of being chosen by unknown wise old men to find secret Tablets that held the secret to saving humanity from being wiped off the face of the map forever. He thought, maybe, I'm suffering from some sort of delusional symptoms. Oh, Well, I'm hungry. I'm going to chalk this one up to my imagination. Noah stopped off at a small diner where he grabbed a bite to eat at the counter next to a colleague and they chatted about inflation.

After an hour, Noah paid the bill and said goodnight to his colleague and began walking home. He was intrigued with his unexpected visitor and felt more positive about the possibility of travel ahead. The next morning, after Noah arrived on campus, he skipped up the stairs and into the building where his office was located and sat down at his desk. He checked for any new messages and grabbed the materials for his class. He needed to prepare the materials for his class.

He pushed his chair away from the desk and stood up and stretched his arms over his head and took a deep breath and exhaled. As he walked over to the window, he could see the campus that was filled with students and professors scurrying about. The grass was forest green and it was so well manicured that it looked more like carpet. Some of the kids sat on the grass under the weeping willow trees while they studied.

Noah remembered listening to the news when he saw the birds fly by. The news reported that hundreds of birds and bees were dropping dead on the ground in different locations and so far, there weren't any explanations for these sudden losses. Last week, he recalled the news reported that dead fish were washing up along the shores in different countries. Noah was concerned about the environment because every living being, plant, tree, animal, mammal, bird, fish and bees are dependent upon humanity living in harmony with the environment in order to survive.

He left his office and walked up the stairs leading to the entrance of the classroom where he was teaching his students that day. He walked into the classroom and walked over to the podium.

Professor Noah said, "Good Morning." He looked at his students and decided to perform a case study on how many students are aware of their environment and if they kept up with world events. Did they know about the strange phenomenon of fish, birds, and bees dropping dead in unprecedented numbers around the world.

After engaging the students, he found that only a few were aware of what was going on with the fish, birds and bees and the environment. He captured their interest and he asked them to research an environmental issue and write a paper on what they've learned for extra credit. The students were totally into it and excited.

A few weeks later, Noah was approached by the Dean. He was surprised when the Dean informed him that the administration was contacted by an organization who chose to remain anonymous. He was informed that these wealthy donors agreed to fund his request to do research across the oceans in search of artifacts that could possibly bring more proof that the dinosaurs are an important part of ancient history.

Noah was thrilled but also shocked that his request actually had come to fruition. "Your request is approved, Noah," the Dean remarked. "You can wind things up and we'll employ a substitute to finish the semester and before you know it, you'll be landing in a remote area across the oceans," he said.

Noah asked, "So, the donors wish to remain anonymous?" The Dean nodded his head in the affirmative. Noah was curious but elated. He couldn't believe that he got so lucky. He couldn't wait to make the arrangements for his journey. He picked up the phone and called his Broker on Wall Street after he saw anonymous protesters on television marching in front of Wall Street near the large monument of a statue of a huge brown Bull symbolic of the "Bull Market." He couldn't wait to tell his friends and figure out which camping gear he would need. He wasn't going to be staying at a 5 Star hotel.

He messaged his friends to meet him at the pub after work so he could inform them of his adventure. He needed to tell them about the grant and his exciting adventure that was about to come true. He also wanted to let them know that he probably can't call them while he was away, but he'll write because he will have access to a small village.

Noah met his friends at the pub for a cold beer and a game of pool. They had lots of questions for him, but he couldn't say too much because he promised Dr. Lee that he would not reveal their meeting or any of the information that he revealed to Noah. Dr. Lee didn't want to cause people to panic or mock Noah or label him as a conspiracy theorist wearing a tin foil hat. He wanted to protect Noah's impeccable record and his future so he would remain credible.

After a couple of hours, Noah hugged his friends and said he would see them in 2 or 3 months depending on the circumstances. He still had to get home and pack his suitcases and locate his camping gear in the garage and try to minimize his luggage and carry on. He shipped his food supply to the nearby village ahead of time so he wouldn't have to worry about it and mailed it in the care of his arranged cab driver, Solomon. He arranged to have his driver bring it with him to the airport before taking him to his destination. He felt as if he was prepared to venture out on his journey across the oceans into the remote jungles of Africa. Noah sat down and set up prepaid accounts for all his bills and he had his mail held at the post office. He asked his neighbor to water his plants and keep an eye on his house while he traveled. His neighbors told him not to worry. He was fortunate to live in a middle-class neighborhood that families lived in for years and the neighbors knew each other and looked out for each other. Noah felt that he took care of everything that needed to be done before leaving the next day for the airport.

Noah was restless because he was so excited. He felt as if he won the Lottery. At last, he had a stroke of Lady Luck and his dream of traveling to a far away foreign land to explore the artifacts arrived. He thought about his dad and how much he enjoyed telling stories of far away lands. Noah smiled when he saw the toy dinosaur on the shelf that his dad gave to him many years ago. He grabbed a book and walked outside and sat in the old red wooden rocking chair that his dad or mom enjoyed in the afternoons during the summertime before dinner.

The Mission Begins

Noah wanted assurance that his investments were secure before he ventured off across the oceans. Noah was set to leave on his mission. Noah was about to leave when he heard the news reported that there was an increasing and unprecedented number of U.S. soldiers dying on the battlefields and committing suicide in the Middle East. He also read that the unemployment and food stamp rates were excessive, but he also realized that nations have good years and good days as well as days that are tragic and call for silent prayers for our heroes and their families. He respected American veterans and U.S. Military heroes and took a moment to pray silently for deceased heroes and their families.

The cab driver showed up on time to take him to the airport, where he checked in and boarded the plane that would fly him to his destination. The flight would take 17 hours, so he settled in and relaxed on the plane. Noah slept during the flight when he wasn't reading a book or watching movies. After the long flight, the moment finally came when the pilot announced they were about to land on the ground. They needed to buckle up. Before landing, Noah looked out the window and he saw a small airport landing and prayed that they would land safely. He felt uneasy and said a prayer.

Suddenly, the plane bounced several times as they touched down on the small runway. Noah's heart dropped a few times. Fortunately, they landed safely and when the plane stopped, Noah took a deep breath and sighed as he whispered, "Thank You, God." He unbuckled his belt when the red light turned off and grabbed his carry on and headed off the plane to the baggage area. He arranged to meet his guide at the same area. Noah prayed that the guide showed up. After all, small villages aren't as easy to confirm reservations for tour guides and he wanted to be sure he arrived early and on time.

There were more passengers lined up for baggage than Noah expected. He stood alongside the other passengers lined up at the baggage area where they awaited their suitcases to be taken off the airplane. Noah looked around for the cab driver. He pre-arranged to meet the driver at the luggage area. Noah spotted the cab driver standing off to the side of the crowd holding a large sign with Noah's name written across it. Noah waved him down and the cab driver walked over to Noah and greeted Noah with a smile. He said, "I'll grab your bags. Follow me, Mr. Noah."

Noah obeyed the driver and grabbed his lightweight bike. He followed the driver as they walked briskly through the airport and outside to the cab. Noah was somewhat surprised when he saw the cab. He set his bike next to the cab and removed his backpack from his back. Noah couldn't help from staring at the cab. He shook his head while looking at the rusty old cab with pitted windows and wobbly tires.

Noah laughed aloud, but he didn't complain because he knew he wasn't in the good old USA any longer. Noah looked around and felt excited. He tossed the backpack in the back seat and Solomon set the camping gear in the trunk then tied the bike to the back of the car.

Noah explained to the driver where he wanted to go, but the driver laughed.

He said, "No problem, Mr. Noah. I know exactly where you want to go."

The driver said, "Hop in the back seat, Mr. Noah." Noah jumped into the back seat and shut the door. Once they were on the road, the driver turned around and said, "Mr. Noah, I am Solomon. If you need anything, you can ask anyone in the village to let Solomon know and I'll do what I can. I brought your food supply."

Noah said, "Thanks, Solomon, I appreciate that." Solomon kept driving and said, "I was named after King Solomon. My family worked in the diamond mines." Solomon laughed heartily. He appeared to be a happy fellow. He said, "We built the village with our earnings. We own everything." They were silent for a few minutes then Solomon turned around and said, "I must warn you, Mr. Noah, the area where you're headed is remote. No one in the surrounding villages dares enter that isolated area. It's the sacred burial ground of the dinosaurs. The villagers are very superstitious."

"There are many stories told by the Elders in the villages about the sacred burial grounds of the dinosaurs. The villagers swear that they've seen the spirit of a powerful dinosaur which they refer to as the beast and believe he's still roaming the land. They believe that they must pray and leave sacrifices outside of this area. They don't want the beast to harm them," Solomon remarked. Noah felt excitement run through his veins.

Noah responded to the driver, "Well, thanks for letting me know, but I must spend some time there. I'm a researcher." Solomon remarked, "No problem, Mr. Noah, but be careful. The villagers believe that area of land is cursed."

As they drove to the location, Noah wasn't bothered by the driver's warnings.

The cab driver arrived at Noah's destination after a two-hour drive.

Noah opened the door and had to push it hard before it opened. He stepped out of the cab and grabbed his backpack. The driver jumped out of the cab and walked to the back of the cab and removed the bike and opened the trunk and grabbed Noah's camping gear and food supply. Noah handed him cash in the amount $6.66 plus a tip and thanked him for his help. Solomon thanked him for the tip.

"Oh, and thanks for the advice.," Noah commented.

The driver smiled. His white teeth glistened against his dark skin which added to his great smile. He said, "If you need a ride back to the airport, just follow the trail for three miles into the small village.

Solomon pointed to the trail with his finger and Noah turned to look in that direction. Solomon stated, "It's easy to find. The village is called Kenyaville." Noah stood still while he looked around the area.

Solomon continued, "I visit my grandma in the village every day. My family is from royal blood, so everyone knows who I am. I am a Prince. My dad was a King, but he passed away. My brother is now the King. My cousin is the leader of the village and his name is Odangason. Everyone in the village knows who we are if you need us. Just follow the trail to your right for three miles like in the movie, 'The Wizard of Oz.' Just follow the yellow brick road," Solomon laughed.

Noah said, "Thanks, I'll see you again, Prince Solomon. I'll be riding my bike into the village from time to time." Solomon laughed, "No Problem, Mr. Noah."

Solomon walked to the driver's side of the cab and said, "I'll see you soon. Goody-Bye." He opened the door that squeaked and jumped into the cab and put his arm outside of the open window and waved as the dust blew in the wind.

Noah stood on the road watching Solomon drive away and disappear from sight. The dust was blowing everywhere as he sped off and the wind cleared the clouds of dust from the surrounding area. Noah laughed as he watched the car bouncing down the road and the old worn tires holding on tightly.

Noah looked around and said, "Well, I guess this is it. I'm on my own. I better get started before it gets dark. I need to find a spot to camp out."

Noah took another look around. He didn't see anything or anyone, but he was fascinated with the jungle noises and the sounds that rang out like music to his ears. The jungle birds were singing in the overgrown tall lush trees. He picked up his camping gear and searched for an area to set up the tent that was near some water. This wasn't the time to be useless, so he got to work and found a good spot.

After setting up the tent, he built a fireplace. He was grateful that there wasn't any rain expected during his stay in this remote land so he could keep his documents and his camera and weapons and clothing dry which was very important for the success not only of the mission but for photos and record keeping of the mission. He knew that it would be getting dark and he needed to complete the physical tasks first. He did feel tired, so he decided to sit under a large shady tree and rest. The blue color of the sky resembled the aqua blue waters in the Caribbean. Noah looked around the remote and foreign jungle area. He slowly looked up at the clear blue sky and spotted his challenger. He spotted a Majestic Mountain hidden by the giant old green leaves of the jungle that stood proud and tall. This must be the hidden mountain that he was sent to explore, but his eyes became heavy and he must not fall asleep just yet.

After Noah realized that he was isolated and alone, the jet lag set in and his body felt tired and weak. Noah was hungry, so he managed enough energy to locate his food supply, coffee, tea, and coffee pot. While the coffee was brewing and his food was heating, he laid down on the cot inside his tent to rest and set the alarm on his watch for 10 minutes so he wouldn't fall asleep. He closed his eyes and when the alarm went off, he reluctantly got up and checked on his food. The coffee was ready. The food was heated. He was starved. He ate the macaroni and cheese and dunked a few cookies into his coffee for dessert. He decided to read a book before he fell asleep. It didn't take long before he fell asleep to the whispering sounds of the owls keeping watch.

In the morning, Noah awakened to birds chirping and the monkeys chatting. He fixed his cot and fixed a fresh pot of coffee. Grabbed a towel and soap and walked over to the water fall that trickled from the rocks where he washed up. The ice-cold water was a quick wakeup call. He walked back to the tent and threw on a shirt and pulled up his hiking pants and tightened his belt. He sat down on the cot and pulled up his socks and boots. After grabbing a mug of piping hot coffee, he fixed a hearty breakfast and he was set for the day. Noah cleaned up around the tent because he didn't want to attract any hungry animals. He grabbed his hiking gear and started his adventure in search of the hidden Judeo-Christian Dinosaur Tablets.'

Of course, Noah was anxious to search for ancient artifacts and dinosaur bones, but he didn't know what to expect in this isolated land. Noah spotted a large sturdy stick and decided he would carry the stick for leverage. He also packed a spear, a knife, a rifle, and a handgun for protection. It was important to pack the correct gear. He felt ready to move on. He headed towards the majestic mountain with his backpack strapped to his back. After 30 minutes of walking, he reached the bottom of the mountain trail and he felt fortunate that there was an actual trail that continued along the mountainside. The trail made his hike easier, but after two hours of climbing, he needed to rest and catch his breath. He grabbed a bottle of water and after a few minutes, he began hiking further up the mountain.

Although the time passed quickly, Noah wasn't a man, who felt discouraged, because he understood that explorations didn't always lead to success, but he remained optimistic. So, each day, he would repeat the same routine and he would remember the instructions given to him by the wise old sage. He knew he must do exactly as Dr. Lee instructed him to do as the days turned into weeks. Nonetheless, Noah consistently repeated his routine without any results. He didn't want to exceed the time he was granted for research from the university. Also, his goal was to locate artifacts that he could bring back to the university that might impress the administrators. Obviously, a successful journey could lead to more donations for grants in the future. He believed that it was now possible to obtain more grants.

Sometimes, Noah found himself doubting his own reality. One day, he was trying to be optimistic after he stopped to prepare a fire and cook a quick meal. On occasion, while eating a meal, he'd mumble, "Maybe, I dreamed this mission. Maybe, Dr. Lee was a figment of my imagination. On the other hand, he struggled with the fact that Dr. Lee appeared to be so real."

Noah searched for weeks hoping for clues so he could find the secret cave. After he finished his meal, he felt a presence about him. He looked up and he was shocked. He smiled and uttered, "Maybe, I'm not crazy after all."

Dr. Lee said, "Hello, Noah. I am here to remind you of your mission and to motivate and encourage you. I know you feel a little discouraged, but it's important that you never give up. Men who give up never complete their mission or reach their destiny when they could be very close to achieving their goal. This is your destiny to seek out the legend of how the dinosaurs became depopulated and extinct. This is your destiny. You must keep your passion to find the secret cave."

Noah said, "Dr. Lee, I've truly tried. I searched every day, but I just can't seem to locate the entrance to the secret cave."

"Not to worry," said Dr. Lee. "The Masters believe in you because you are an achiever. You must expand your mind and remember that humanity depends upon you and your success at locating the legend of how the dinosaurs became depopulated or made extinct. This is the reason you were chosen. You have a strong passion for truth and a relentless desire to seek knowledge and share your research with other people so they can learn from the evolving species. Mankind is on the endangered list and they must save themselves by learning from past generations. Although, we are anonymous, we are watching your progress" and once again without warning, Dr. Lee vanished.

Obviously, it wasn't easy hiking up and down the mountainside. In fact, the sun was so hot on some days that it turned Noah's skin to a dark golden brown. Sometimes, Noah thought about returning home, but he would always sleep on his decision. One day, after hiking up and down the mountainside for weeks, he did become discouraged and he began packing up his gear. He felt sad as he jumped on his bike to ride back to the village, but, just as he was about to leave, he looked up at the mountainside and decided to take a few more photographs of the majestic hidden mountain. Noah picked up his professional camera and as he stared into the lens of his camera, he caught a quick glimpse of what appeared to be an opening on the side of the mountain. He stopped in his tracks. He stood still and stared at the opening. He said, "What is that? Could that be the hidden cave on the side of the mountain?" Of course, he thought that his eyes were playing tricks on him. He asked, "How is it possible that I never saw that opening before?"

At that moment, Noah thought he heard Dr. Lee's voice whisper in his ear, "Noah, your hard work will be rewarded. Never give up. Men who give up their dreams because they didn't go the extra mile can never win the race."

Noah felt a surge of adrenaline running through his veins. He dropped his camping gear, except for his backpack, and left his bike on the ground next to a tree. He grabbed his hiking stick and he began hiking back up the mountainside so he could check out what appeared to be the secret cave.

His heart started to beat faster with each step as he neared the opening. Noah was so excited that he began whistling along the trail. He whistled the song, Hi Ho Hi Ho it's off to work we go with each step.

Of course, Noah's emotions were running wild with curiosity. He continued to hike without stopping to rest except when he couldn't hike any further. But, he was determined to reach his destination. At last, Noah arrived. He spotted the opening built into the cave.

"It must be the cave! This is it. Dr. Lee, this must be the cave." Yes, this must be the cave! This is it. Dr. Lee, this must be the cave!," he cried out. His voice echoed throughout the mountainside and rang out joyously. He hoped it was the same cave that Dr. Lee told him that he needed to locate. Step by step, he cautiously walked inside the dark cold cave. He stopped so he could light a lantern. He placed a hard hat on his head and turned on a flashlight attached to it.

As Noah was digesting everything he could see in the cave, it was so awesome and untouched by man. He felt as if he was experiencing a touch of heaven. The cave was awesome and took his breath away. The beauty inside the cave inspired him as he witnessed the beautiful rainbow of colors dazzling inside on the walls and ceiling. Noah said, "This is amazing. I've never seen such brilliant colors." He stared at the frozen stalactites hanging from the ceilings in all different shapes and sizes untouched by mankind. The waterfall flowed down the side of the rocks into the pool of water that picked up the colorful rainbows reflecting off the water that made it appear as if one was staring at glass Streams of water trickled through the cracks in the rocks flowing into the pool of water.

He admired the unusual tropical plants protruding between the rocks of the cave. Noah walked over to the pool and touched the water. He sat down on a rock near the pool and decided to just take it all in before exploring. He wanted to sit and rest for awhile and snack. He sat on a camping cushion and poured hot coffee from a thermos and grabbed a sandwich and decided to sketch his first impression of the cave.

A sketch pad was inside his backpack, so he reached for it and located the sketch pad and the pencils. He sat down and began sketching the inside of the cave. He enjoyed art when he was in high school and college and enjoyed sketching in his spare time at home. It relaxed him and took him away from reality. He wanted to sketch the cave as he saw it and experienced by his hands as a personal memory of what he witnessed.

29

CHAPTER 4

Professor Noah vs. Professor Obamasaurus

The temptation for Noah to splash his face and hands was overwhelming, so he indulged and refreshed himself. He searched for a rock with a hollow center to collect the water so his human hands never touched the water inside the pool. It worked for him. He resisted for a few minutes enjoying the cool breeze and the meditative sounds of the waterfall and the echoes from the drops of water.

The cave was so magnificent and untouched that he felt his mind was not able to comprehend the beauty created by nature. Noah decided that it wouldn't be a good idea to take photos of the stalactites that might disturb the natural beauty with film or flashing lights that may damage what nature has protected since ancient times.

Noah did photograph the unusual and colorful tropical ferns that bloomed with gorgeous flowers and colors that he had never seen before even though he's traveled to tropical islands. The tropical plants and flowers emitted the most sensual and warm fragrances that superseded that of Red Roses, Gardenias, Sweet Honeysuckle and Lilacs. This truly was a cave of beauty and an unknown wonder of the world. Noah felt invigorated. He stood up and walked further inside the cave.

After standing up and stretching, he held up the lantern near the walls of the mountain in search of any artifacts or carved photos or unusual symbols and writings. As he slowly and carefully examined the walls of the cave, he suddenly stopped in his tracks. He nearly tripped over something. He lowered the lantern and looked down to see what he stumbled upon. He was shocked.

It appears that he tripped over petrified dinosaur bones. They appeared to be the bones of two young adult male dinosaurs from their size and shape. Were these two young male dinosaurs hiding in the cave and left behind. Noah was excited and quietly said, "Maybe this is it. Maybe, there really is a Legend of the Judeo-Christian Dinosaurs left behind by the dinosaurs who may have been hiding out in this cave from danger.

Noah pulled a second lantern out of his backpack and created more light. He pulled out his flashlight and began shining the light on the walls in search of the carved writings. He was impressed with a myriad of precious stones imbedded into the rocks inside of the cave as he continued his search. Noah felt certain that he would discover rare artifacts and clues. He realized that his destiny was to discover the untold and ancient history of the legend, but what was the message he needed to discover so he could bring that message back to America?

As the lights from the lantern flickered, he thought he saw engraved symbols or pictures carved in stone along the walls, but he wasn't sure. His search for locating the Tablets had just begun, but it was getting late.

Noah lost track of time. Finally, he mumbled, "I need to rest, I'm really tired. Maybe, I'll just head back to camp." A little sadness struck him because he didn't want to leave, but he knew he should get back to camp, just to be safe. Fortunately, just as Noah headed back towards the opening of the cave, he suddenly stopped. He wasn't sure what he saw. He began walking towards another wall on his way out of the cave. He noticed strange symbols and strange writings carved into the wall.

He studied the carved stones for a few minutes and realized that he may be staring at something rare. Noah was intrigued once again with this unusual adventure. The excitement of the moment was inevitable knowing that he may have discovered at least part of the ancient dinosaur Tablets that Dr. Lee instructed him to locate. One of the carvings appeared to be a carving of a magnificent dinosaur.

Noah couldn't contain himself. He was overwhelmed with such a find. The thought of dinosaurs roaming these mountain tops and jungles brought him back to his childhood when he would drag out the myriad of dinosaurs he had collected as a child from his old wooden toy box and use his imagination and pretend that he could ride on the dinosaurs. Pet them. Talk to them. Admire their powerful size and bodies and their strength. Even though dinosaurs had a very small brain, they had great instincts and Noah thinks they were more intelligent than Scientists believe.

He also found 2 petrified dinosaur bones in another part of the cave. They were lying near the dinosaur Tablets. They appeared to be the bones of elderly male dinosaurs. Noah was pretty certain that those 2 male dinosaurs may have been the elders who may have etched the "Legend of How the Judeo-Christian Dinosaurs Became Extinct" using symbols to carve their legend into stone for future species to decipher and as acknowledgement of their existence.

"This must be it," Noah shouted with excitement repeatedly inside the cave. His shouting rang out and echoed throughout the cave, He exclaimed, "This is it! This must be it!" Noah laughed aloud. He couldn't believe that the Tablets clearly named the magnificent dinosaur to be Obamasaurus. This was the name that he had given to his special toy dinosaur when his dad gave him the toy on his 7th Birthday as he wondered if it was just a coincidence.

Noah wondered if these events are coincidences or destiny. After all, how could there be so many coincidences from my childhood into my adult years involving my interest in the dinosaur world leading to Dr. Lee and this remote secret cave and the Legend with a secret message to save humanity, he pondered.

His eyes felt teary eyed. He chuckled hysterically. Noah listened to music on his audio plugged into his ears. He loudly cried out, "Dr. Lee, Dr. Lee, I think I found the ancient dinosaur tablets." He began to perspire. His hands felt sweaty. His heart was beating faster and faster. He reached inside of his backpack and grabbed a very expensive thick black brush kept inside a box.

The brush was made to carefully brush away dirt or dust from artifacts, so they aren't damaged. His hands shook as he mumbled, "I hope these are the 2 elderly dinosaurs that carved the legend." Noah decided to leave before dark and come back in the morning. It was a long walk down the mountainside.

After an exciting day of organizing his plan for the following day, Noah headed back to camp and rested until the next morning. He thought, good grief, this is my Birthday, September 11th, 2008. Noah always spent a moment remembering the Americans who were murdered by radical terrorists on September 11, 2001. Although, Noah wasn't a religious guy, he was very spiritual. He always thanked God for allowing him to wake up every morning and for giving him one more day to continue on his mission. He thought, this is the best birthday gift, I could ever wish for. He said, "Thank you, Lord. If only I could thank Dr. Lee."

Noah was fascinated as to how the dinosaurs were able to survive upon the earth for millions of years. He also had an interest in natural organic foods and anti-aging products. He didn't approve of GMO's manufactured without any nutritional value and believed in planting God's seeds.

In fact, he didn't approve of chemicals and unnecessary preservatives injected into animals and foods which humans consume. He believed that God provided everything we need upon the earth to keep the immune system healthy. The many groups that Noah supported included people concerned about the adverse side effects from the myriad of chemicals and preservatives and toxic poisons that are leaked into the environment. The sky. Soil. Water. Food. Household Products. Cosmetics. Vaccines. Rx Drugs. Toxic Oil Spills. Fluoride. Radiation.

He wondered why so many people were suffering from rashes and allergies, cancer and respiratory illnesses that have continued increasing in America and should have decreased. After all, the American people donate Billions to Big Pharma Research and Development and NIH for and R&D in Labs at Universities and yet, cancer and heart attacks, Influenza, and Diabetes remain major causes of death.

Time was not on Noah's side even though he forged ahead to make the most of his time, but he had to leave before dark and get back to camp.

Fortunately, Noah was strong. He could endure climbing up and down the mountainside. After he grabbed his backpack and his walking stick, he headed out of the cave and back to his campsite. He wanted to be rested and refreshed when he continued with his investigation of the cave the next day. He hoped he would find the answers he was searching for so he would not fail on his first expedition. After he arrived at the campsite, he took out a mirror to see how thick his beard had grown. He noticed the worry lines across his forehead, but they just added to his character. In fact, he was quite handsome and rugged in appearance. He stood tall and strong.

Noah would never think of himself as a model on the cover of an outdoor magazine. In fact, his female friends mentioned that he could easily model, but he just laughed it off. He wasn't interested in publicity. He preferred living a quiet life and working at what he enjoyed. He was blessed with thick wavy salt and pepper hair. Big Sparkling Blue Eyes. And a smile that lit up the room. His nose was a little crooked, Noah's jaw appeared strong and chiseled.

His expensive professional camera and equipment was handled very carefully and placed with care inside the backpack. He wanted to make sure that he would be ready to photograph the unseen secrets of the Judeo-Christian Dinosaur Tablets.

"I think I have everything I need to document what I discover," he commented. He felt he needed to prove what he discovered in order to convince donors to fund more expeditions in the future.

Noah wondered why the 2 petrified eggs were left behind. Is it possible that there were heterosexual dinosaurs hidden away in the cave and trying to save their baby dinosaur eggs? After all, it took a male and female to procreate baby dinosaurs. He wondered what happened that the petrified eggs were left behind and not hatched and if the mother and father's dinosaur bones were somewhere in the different halls of the cave, but he didn't want to venture too far into the cave and get trapped or get lost in case he needed to get out quickly. He didn't want his bones petrified.

After he arrived back at the camp. Noah lit a fire and searched for a can of soup. He poured a can of soup into a tin pot. Heated it on the fire. He brewed a cup of coffee and rested. He grabbed a cup of soup and threw in some oyster crackers in his bowl. He wanted to get a goodnight sleep. He was starving and he gobbled down the entire can of soup and enjoyed some cheese and fruit on the side.

After all, it wasn't every day that he would be photographing the bones of ancient dinosaurs or petrified dinosaur eggs. There wasn't any doubt in his mind that this was a once in a lifetime opportunity. He made sure that he was prepared for the morning. He made a list to check off every day before hiking up the mountain because he couldn't just come back down and do it again. He knew he must be careful to take everything he needed with him because time was not on his side. Noah was extremely tired after such a long day. He quickly crawled into his cot and sighed after he laid his long body on the cot and his head hit the pillow. It didn't take long once he laid down to fall into a deep sleep.

Petrified Dinosaur Egg

The next day, Noah didn't waste any time. He drank his coffee and ate a hearty breakfast and packed up and headed back to the cave. It was a pleasant climb because the sun was just beginning to rise. Once he arrived at the cave, he photographed, the tropical plants and the petrified dinosaur bones, but he still didn't photograph the stalactites. Noah knew that flashing lights might harm them similar to original paintings in a museum where flash cameras are prohibited.

As Noah explored deeper into the cave, he saw something on another wall, so he got out his flashlight from the side of his backpack and shined the light on the area that caught his eye. To his surprise, he located 2 rare artifacts.

These had never been found. He was so excited. He said, "I can't believe it. Could this be true?" There they were right before his eyes. Two more petrified dinosaur eggs.

Noah's hands were shaking as he reached for his camera from his backpack. I must take perfect pictures of these rare finding so I can prove that they really exist. He adjusted his camera and tried to keep his hands steady while he took the photos of the dinosaur eggs to bring back to America. He didn't touch the eggs for fear of damaging them.

The fact that the 2 petrified eggs were left behind left him curious and wondering if they had heterosexual dinosaurs hidden away in the caves because in America there were Liberal wealthy investors seeking to reduce the population. They had been targeting Christians, Catholics, Jews, Traditional Marriage and Traditional Families since 1993. Heterosexuals and Judeo-Christians believe in procreation, but they did not. He wondered what happened that the petrified eggs were left behind and not hatched by the mother dinosaur which remained a mystery to Noah. The petrified dinosaur eggs were a rare treasure.

Afterwards, Noah pulled out his journal from his backpack and began writing dates, times, locations, and personal notes about his adventure and discoveries. He kept excellent notes because his notes had to be accurate in order to be believed when he returned home. Noah also drew the symbols from the Legend of the Dinosaur Tablets so that he could provide those symbols as well to his colleagues and students.

Noah laid back on his backpack leaning against the rocks. He kept hydrated with plenty of water and chewed on strips of beef jerky and large protein bars or mixed nuts. Fresh tropical fruits were plentiful. The tropical fruits grew everywhere in the jungle and a wonderful sight to behold as they were 100% natural. The bananas were his favorite.

Noah snacked on his food while his imagination went wild. He imagined giant muscular dinosaurs roaming the earth for Billions of years without fear of competition. He thought about the fearless giants that dominated the earth, which made him feel confused because it wasn't clear how such giant creatures could become an endangered species and end up depopulated and made extinct. This one question haunted him and continued to linger in his mind. What if they weren't extinct?

The reason Noah was so disturbed by the fact that these giant dinosaurs could be made extinct from the planet needed an explanation as far as he was concerned. He believed that if the dinosaurs could be made extinct or depopulated then he figured that it is possible for humanity to be made extinct or depopulated.

After all, the government can access Nukes, HAARP, Chemtrails, Radiation, EMP's and Microwaves which can exterminate people. And, the American people don't have a clue what secret high-tech weapons that the military and government or Wall Street have developed or even foreign nations that could wipe out all of humanity. Although, Noah didn't view himself as a conspiracy theorist which Liberals claim is a buzz word for being "crazy" because people question the government or Science limits the ability to expand the mind.

As Noah's mind wandered, he thought about the immigrants who migrated into the United States of America and the myriad of American Indian tribes that existed at that time, but some tribes were depopulated by European immigrants, who believe Native Americans were non-humans. The bigots believed that certain minorities were non-humans and if they didn't fit the stereotype in the minds of the Bigots or those with prejudice in their hearts and minds then they should be aborted or starved or used as slaves for hard labor or exterminated which occurred.

Of course, there were good people who didn't agree with prejudice and opposed bigotry. The history books confirm that many tribes of the Native Americans in the USA were made extinct. The history books are filled with tribes of ethnic people or races that were made extinct when their nations were conquered by foreign enemies.

The many Native American tribes that were made extinct by immigrants who based the decisions on greed targeted those tribes. They were forced off their rich farmlands where they grew crops and had a water supply. They killed off the abundant Buffalo that the Native Americans only killed for blankets and coats and food, but the immigrants killed them for profit. The Native Americans forced off their land either froze to death or died of dehydration or starved to death. So, yes, Noah thought, ethnic people and entire nations can be depopulated and made extinct. In fact, Canada's government ordered all Native American children be removed from their parent's custody and placed in Canadian schools to be reprogrammed, but instead the parents weren't allowed any contact with their children and the children were abused and raped and many died.

Although, Canada and U.S. History books have attempted to conceal this from the public, the truth always finds a way to be revealed. Unfortunately, the truth can't bring back those who were murdered or made extinct because by the time the truth reaches the ears of good people who seek justice, the suspects who committed the abuses are usually dead. Sometimes, wrongs take decades to make right.

Noah sighed. He said, "Could that happen to other human beings in America today? After all, there are wealthy greedy global leaders who believe it's a good thing to depopulate the planet. He wondered if the U.S. Natural Born Citizen should be placed on the endangered species list. It's no secret that the goal of the globalists is depopulation and ethnic and religious and political cleansing.

Depopulation kept creeping into Noah's mind as he remembered how evil globalist accomplished depopulating people throughout history. The evil ones exude narcissism and appear to be psychopaths without conscience. Psychopaths are charismatic, successful, and they thrive on power and control, and justify their abuses to be for the better good of others.

Noah thought about World War II and how one evil tyrannical leader, Adolph Hitler, could form an army of young healthy Nazi males who were trained to be tyrants and carry out heinous crimes against humanity. They tattooed the arms of those they took hostage as their property or chattel and slaves who they forced into servitude. They reprogrammed their youth into believing that Jews and many others were non-humans and disposable and viewed as obsolete and of no value to the Nazi government.

Noah was recalling stories of extermination. Hitler depopulated a total of 11,000,000 Jews and other human beings or more. (some people say the number murdered was closer to 50,000,000 people) before America sent troops to rescue the Jews and Europeans who survived the WW II Holocaust.

The goal once again was to exterminate the Jews and all who didn't fit the stereotype of a superior race. Hitler's doctors and Scientists happily joined in and performed experimental and trial injections and surgeries on those they took hostage and used radiation and chemicals to sterilize young people. Hitler and his army committed Crimes against Humanity. Afterwards, the Nuremberg Codes declared it a Crime against Humanity to use human beings as human lab rats and mandated a death sentence for those charged and found guilty.

Noah stood up and jogged a little and stretched. The journey was not what he expected to find or discover. The wonders of the world made him realize how little the world knows about the past living species and space. After all, the world is evolving every day with new entities coming to life and many being made extinct. And, with today's modern technology for cures, he wondered how is it that the death tolls and illnesses aren't improving health, but many treatments using chemo or lasers or microwaves aren't ending the long list of serious health effects on human beings.

Noah mumbled, "How could anyone believe that creating fear with the goal of depopulating a race or religion is in the best interest of humanity?" He thought silently and wondered if there could be an evil force conspiring to wipe out humanity as many believe or is it all propaganda? He whispered, "One thing is for sure, if true, it's pure evil." He took a few deep breaths and exhaled and relaxed his mind. The history books and documentaries and books are filled with stories of psychopaths and serial killers who justify their criminal thinking and actions by telling themselves that the victims deserve to be wiped out and it's for the benefit of society.

As he looked around the cave, he spotted an unusual artifact that caught Noah's attention. He couldn't believe what he discovered. He thought for a moment in disbelief. There can't be two more dinosaur eggs petrified inside these rocks. He wondered if there were even more hidden away. He again thought about how people hid pregnancy and babies from the Nazi army or how Communist China forced 40,000,000 women to abort their female babies during the 1990's.

Noah switched his thoughts as if he pulled a light switch on and off. He couldn't help but think about the dinosaurs. There wasn't just one species of dinosaurs. Of course there would be good and evil dinosaurs and jealous dinosaurs. Obviously, the dinosaur world included a myriad of species that evolved into various sizes, colors, and forms. Noah compared the height of the dinosaurs to that of the Twin Towers in New York City.

The Twin Towers stood tall and mighty just like the dinosaurs that stood tall and mighty. They touched the clouds. The Twin Towers and 3,000 Americans were wiped out in a matter of minutes on 9/11/2001. If it had been an attack with a nuke, millions would have died, so yes, people can be depopulated. Millions of babies have been depopulated in America and China. And, the majestic dinosaurs were also wiped off the face of the map, but by whom and why and how were the questions that Noah could not stop asking himself.

Americans shouldn't place 100% trust in their taxpayer funded leaders, because it's We The People who are used and abused when government officials go rogue and suddenly declare themselves to be totalitarian dictators and attempt to force the majority of their citizens to comply with unlawful, illegal or unconstitutional laws that can harm them and their loved ones should they commit Crimes against Humanity.

The fact that the U.S. government failed to detect planes that were flying outside of America's air space bothered Noah. He realized that all creatures have the choice to remain vigilant against enemy attacks or be passive and remain vulnerable to evil agendas. They can choose to participate in evil deeds or they can choose to fight back against evil deeds.

Professor Noah realized the importance of not touching the artifacts without wearing gloves. He was determined to search and locate as many of the Dinosaur Tablets as possible. Noah was excited and had the passion to continue with his mission and not give up is remarkable. He used his time to gather as much information as he could as well as document as much as possible. Noah carried his journal with him so he could keep notes as well as his sketch pad. Noah respected the historical artifacts that he believed must be preserved for future generations.

CHAPTER 5

The Dinosaur Tablets

It became clear to Noah that there wasn't just one dinosaur Tablet, but a compilation of Tablets carved over time that would make up an entire collection. Noah felt satisfied that this discovery was evidence that his dream on that hot summer night about his mission was real. He was glad that his meeting with Dr. Lee, the mystical elder's appearances were real, not an illusion.

Afterwards, Noah sat on a flat rock and studied the carvings engraved in stone and attempted to unravel "The Legend of How the Judeo-Christian Dinosaur Nation Became Extinct." He knew it wouldn't be easy to decode the Tablets. Of course, he was aware that his discovery would be that of rare and ancient symbols. He acknowledged that any artifacts he discovered would be considered a rare and priceless ancient treasure. The reality that he may discover the unseen hidden message from the leader of the Judeo-Christian Dinosaur Nation would be considered a priceless treasure. The fact that he discovered so many clues led him to believe that he may have discovered the hidden legend which could help mankind survive an impending crisis that could exterminate human beings by altering their minds.

After thinking about his discovery, he decided that most researchers and scientists are interested in the brain which sparked a note in Noah's head. The fact that the dinosaurs lived for millions of years and grew to be giants roaming the earth led Noah to believe that their brains were a major part of the puzzle to their longevity. He realized that it's a no brainer that dinosaurs lived healthy lives because they weren't eating or drinking or breathing chemicals and toxins into their bodies and they weren't exposed to radiation except from the sun's safe natural rays emitting vitamin D3 that kept their immune system strong.

After all, man-made chemicals or nuclear power plants or technology emitting radiation around the clock that can harm living species didn't exist.

The weather was controlled by God and Mother Nature, not controlled or manipulated by manmade technology such as triangulation, HAARP or chemtrails used by government agencies or funded by wealthy men invested in Wall Street.

The fact that governments secretly used human beings who are used as guinea pigs or human lab rats for the government and Big Pharma's medical experiments and trials with unknown consequences immediately or down the road. The thought that Individuals can experience death or permanent injury frightened Noah. There were rumors secretly whispered that a mad Scientist developed technology to inject into the human body that would turn human beings into mindless zombies that appears to be part of a fictional Sci-fi movie, but now he pondered if it was fictional Sci-fi or reality.

As Noah's brain digested the information he was considering in depth, he decided that most nations are destroyed or overthrown because of the failure of men and women who are weak. They sell out the country for the material world. Noah packed up his gear as he was getting closer to deciphering the Tablets and uncovering the legend. He headed back to camp so he could eat dinner and get to bed.

Dr. Le Fauccini: The Mad Scientist

The following morning, Noah couldn't wait to return to the cave so he got up before sunrise and prepared his breakfast. Enjoyed 2 cups of coffee with 4 lumps of sugar and a little powdered creamer. He poured the rest of the coffee in the coffee pot into a stainless steel thermos and packed up his lunch and snack and the tools he needed and headed out to start his day with a clear mind.

After the long climb, he entered the cave and set up his professional equipment. Noah settled down and got to work decoding the legend carved into the dinosaur Tablets that were dated 2008 B.C.

The Legend fascinated Noah from the start as it began with a description of the secret Sacred Gardens. As he began to decipher the legend, he visualized the Sacred Gardens in his mind. He wanted to live in the legend not just decipher it which created a movie in his mind.

Noah decoded that in the beginning God created a magnificent male dinosaur named Dinoman.

As a child, Dinoman used his energy and time to romp about the Sacred Gardens where God allowed him to live a carefree life. He could swim, run, stroll through the gardens, and he could talk to God. But, as the years passed, Dinoman grew to be 20 feet tall. A magnificent muscular specimen, indeed, but he was the only giant roaming about the Sacred Gardens. But, despite his size, God considered him to be a gentle dinosaur and God was pleased with his creation. Dinoman's big hazel eyes twinkled every time he spotted beautiful sweet fruits or healthy green leaves. Dinoman felt safe and secure whenever God spoke to him. His thick lips and big teeth created an irresistible smile and his eyes twinkled with innocence.

Dinoman's enormous size and his charisma helped him feel empowered and confident. He didn't fear Mother Nature because he was protected from harm while he lived in God's Sacred Gardens.

But, Dinoman matured. He started feeling lonely. One day, God asked, "Dinoman, why are you so sad?" Dinoman said, "I'm lonely. I don't have a companion." God loved Dinoman very much. God decided to remove Dinoman's loneliness. God granted his request without telling Dinoman. God wanted to surprise him. One clear night while Dinoman was sleeping soundly, God decided to surprise him the next morning. God created a female dinosaur. God was pleased with his new female creature that he created from the rib of Dinoman. He named her, Dinawoman.

The next morning the sun was shining brightly when Dinoman awakened. He was surprised and curious about the new friend. He immediately became starry eyed and bashful when Dinawoman woke up and looked at him and smiled. They immediately became friends and the two young dinosaurs decided to give each other a nickname. Dinoman said, "I will call you Dina and you call me Dino" and from that day forward, the two dinosaurs were inseparable.

God gave them specific instructions about the Sacred Gardens. He also warned them not to wander into certain areas or they would be punished. He warned them that they were to be kind and respectful of each other, but they were free to play and splash in the crystal like lakes and eat fresh fruits and leaves from the gardens. They were warned that they were never to eat from the tree of knowledge that kept the secrets of good and evil. So, all appeared well in the sacred gardens at that time and the 2 young dinosaurs wanted for nothing.

It was common for God to check on His 2 creations that he breathed life into so they could live upon the earth. He created fresh and clean air before he created the earth so all living species could survive upon the earth. God created what He coined as the "Breath of Life." It is the fresh clean air that keeps all living species upon the earth alive. God checked on his 2 magnificent creations from time-to-time to make sure that they were happy and content with life. God warned them that they could eat from any of the trees and plants, but that they were forbidden to eat from the Tree of Knowledge. If they did, they would be cursed and punished.

He created everything they needed to be happy and content living in the Sacred Gardens. The 2 young dinosaurs didn't know anything about working or providing for themselves. They took the Sacred Gardens for granted. They remained in God's good graces and were spared any pain and suffering. They were protected by God and they never had to worry about hunger or thirst.

Dina was smitten with Dino and she fantasized about him as her hero. Dino taught her how to stay safe and which plants and fruits she could eat and which foods she shouldn't eat. He also taught her how to swim in the deep waters so they could splash about on sunny days. She only had eyes for Dino.

Super Obamasaurus

After a few months, Dino noticed that Dina was built with a frail beautiful body and a lighter more delicate skin which he hadn't noticed before. She had big brown Bambi eyes with long thick lashes. Her pink lips were thick and heart shaped. Dino fell head over heels for her, so he wanted to please her. Together, they lived a fairy tale life hidden away from any harm. Dino and Dina enjoyed strolling through the colorful floral gardens filled with warm and sensual fragrances such as vanilla and sandalwood. They enjoyed the good life.

They picked their organic fresh fruits and a variety of different types of berries right off the vine, which were plump, juicy, and sweet as honey. God had warned Dino and Dina not to eat from the mystical tree, but Dina believed she was a feminist and she believed in liberalism after she listened to a reptilian species that crawled up to her and told her that they could be gods if they ate from the tree of knowledge. Dina believed the reptilian and she disobeyed God. She knew Dino was weak and couldn't resist her beauty, so she convinced Dino to do the same. Dino submitted and took a bite of the forbidden fruit, but they didn't feel empowered or feel like gods. They suddenly knew they had disobeyed God for the first time and tried to hide from God.

But after Dino took the first bite of the forbidden fruit, he felt emotions that he had never known before. He realized that they angered God. God asked, "Where are you? Come out and show yourselves immediately. Dino and Dina were scared for the first time in their lives. Dino blamed Dina and Dina blamed the reptilian snake who tempted her to disobey God. Suddenly, they felt their bodies tremble with fear. God said, "What have you done?" You touched the forbidden Tree of Life. You sinned against me. Now, I must command you to leave the Sacred Gardens for I cannot tolerate sin. Dina and Dino asked forgiveness and they told God they were sorry.

God was sad, but he knew that they must be tested. He told them he loved them and forgave them, but they could no longer live in the Sacred Gardens, but must live in the world where there is good and evil and be tested and prove their sorrow by doing good deeds. God cast them out of the Sacred Gardens. God chose to punish Dino and Dina and cast them out and for the first time, Dino and Dina were embarrassed when they realized their physical differences. God instructed them to cover themselves with fig leaves. This was the first time Dino and Dina realized shame. He informed them that they would enter into a land where they would have to search for an area near water and trees.

They would spend their lives building villages and a nation that required shelter, food, herbs, and water to protect themselves from the unknown elements. He instructed them not to disobey God again.

As Dino and Dina matured, God noticed that they were smitten with each other. God commanded them to bond as one and marry in front of God and all he created upon the earth. He instructed them to follow his commandment to love one another as they love themselves so the world can live in peace when more babies are born. God told Dina that since she was the cause of the sin that she would bare many baby dinosaurs in pain and suffering, but they would bring her and Dino joy and love and help them maintain their village as Dino and Dina grew old and wise.

God commanded them to be fruitful and fill the earth with more dinosaurs so that they could establish sovereign nations and the young dino-men could be trained to protect and defend their homes and families and nation. He instructed Dino to protect his wife and baby dinosaurs and in return, Dina would respect and love him until they died. He commanded that marriage was to be between one male dinosaur and one female dinosaur so that they could procreate upon the earth for generations to come and establish their sovereign nations. This is not what the reptilian snake wanted to happen upon the earth, so he sought to depopulate God's creations.

After one year, Dino and Dina were blessed with twin boys. In fact, Dina gave birth to twelve baby dinosaurs over the years including two sets of twins. As their offspring reached maturity, they married and procreated. After many years, the dinosaurs ruled the earth. The population of dinosaurs increased substantially upon the earth. They were instructed to plow the fields so they could grow more fruit trees and provide a variety of berries and herbs.

Dino instructed the dinosaurs to always build their villages near water and near trees and plants that were plentiful. As time passed, the dinosaurs continued to have large families who could then help with the difficult chores needed to be done in the villages. It appeared that the hard work and good deeds of Dino and Dina paid off because the dinosaurs were thriving and feared by smaller creatures that evolved and God forgave them and protected them, but they were not free from all evil.

Curiosity killed the cat, but Noah's curiosity got the best of him. He spent most of his time working to decode the dinosaur Tablets. His ability to decipher the symbols became easier as if he was decoding a foreign language or ancient scrolls. Noah lost all track of time and hunger struck like a clock. He found delight in the fact the dinosaurs were Judeo-Christians and believed in heterosexuality and one male and one female bonding so they could procreate and keep their species alive.

The dinosaurs had creative minds that led to the invention of tools and weapons made from rocks and metals and wood that they gathered from their natural surroundings. They felt that if they invented these tools and weapons that they could not only build walls to protect their villages, but they could protect themselves from harm should the forces of nature turn against them. In fact, they built an outdoor Town Hall where they could gather on occasion and participate in social events or meet to discuss important issues of the day.

The Tablets revealed that the Elder who ruled the Dinosaur nation was named Dinomoses. It was Dinomoses who appeared to have built the Judeo-Christian Dinosaur Nation exuding himself as a leader since his childhood. One day, Dinomoses felt that he had to speak out. Dinomoses informed his fellow dinosaurs that he had a very real and prophetic dream. Of course, everyone was curious and wanted to hear about his dream. The dinosaurs gathered and encouraged him as he listened to their voices echoing, "Tell us about the dream, Dinomoses."

Dinomoses tightened his lips as if in deep thought and then said, "I dreamed that one day in the future, God would send his Only Begotten Son to live upon the earth and he would teach and preach the good news to the nations so the earth could be fruitful and prosperous and every species could live healthy lives if they followed God's Ten Commandments."

Dinomoses spoke in a convincing and firm tone and told the dinosaurs that even though God's Son would be born sometime in the future that if the dinosaurs professed their belief in God, and ask forgiveness for any misdeeds that God would establish a Judeo-Christian Dinosaur Nation and bless their land with milk and honey. He said to keep looking up at the skies at night and watch for the stars to give a sign. Thereafter, the Judeo-Christian dinosaurs formed groups. The key group was named, the "Tree Party." A second group formed and called themselves, the "Oath Seekers." The Oath Seekers swore to uphold the dinosaur's supreme laws and protect their nation's borders from foreign enemies. The "Tree Party" was protective of the natural environment and preserving the laws and traditions of the Judeo Christian Dinosaur Nation.

Obviously, the dinosaurs were dependent upon a secure and healthy environment which was very important to their survival. The elders were respected for their wisdom and the elders were the leaders of the Judeo-Christian Dinosaur Nation. The dinosaurs believed in a Judeo-Christian God as their creator, but there was a group of atheist dinosaurs who did not believe in God and they formed their secret society and met in secret.

The dinosaur Framers who created and carved the constitutional laws into stone guaranteed Freedom, Liberty, Rights, Sovereignty, and Justice for All.

The "Tree Party" stood up as dinosaur activists and believed that the supreme laws established by the Framers of the dinosaur world who risked their lives must be preserved. So, the dinosaurs lived by their dinosaur Rule of Law, formed a Republic, and established a sovereign nation led by elected dinosaurs who established laws that protected the welfare and safety of the Dinosaur Nation based on a Judeo-Christian foundation.

Noah figured out that the dinosaurs instinctively guarded the Dinosaur nation from anti-dinosaur enemies. They protected the unborn dinosaurs.

They believed in the sanctity of life. God warned the dinosaurs that they must protect their Judeo-Christian Dinosaur Nation or they could be seduced by an evil reptilian creature. He warned that the reptilian creature will suddenly appear in their Judeo-Christian land and he'll be welcomed as a charismatic and benevolent creature. He'll present himself as one of them, but he isn't one of them. In fact, he intends to do harm. God said that the reptilian dinosaur might say, "I am the one. I am God. I shall be exalted above all nations," and many Judeo-Christian dinosaurs will be seduced by his false promises. God warned that many dinosaurs will worship him and pray to him and follow his mandates. The Elders believed that the reptilian creature will be difficult to identify or stop.

God warned that the reptilian creature will come through the back door unexpectedly while the dinosaurs sleep. He will be a foreigner born on foreign soil and lived in anti-Judeo-Christian nations, where violent acts against their own dinosaur citizens and even dinosaur kids were viewed as honorable. He will brainwash the Judeo-Christian dinosaurs to believe that they should be tolerant of violent acts under the guise of religion. The reptilian creature will promote political correctness which is the catalyst he intends to use to silence all dinosaurs who oppose his agendas.

The reptilian dinosaurs would justify their crimes against humanity as protected under their foreign ideologies. The Judeo-Christian dinosaurs were warned that the reptilian will seduce their nation by promising to bring hope and change and transformation. The reptilian dinosaur will confuse millions of Judeo-Christian dinosaurs into believing what is wrong is right and what is right is wrong. He will have a slick tongue that could turn the lies into truth. Millions of Judeo-Christian dinosaurs will believe he is the one and they shall bow and pray to the false prophet.

The Tablets read that God warned the dinosaurs that the reptilian dinosaur would promise many wonderful things, but his real intent would be to lead them away from their Judeo-Christian beliefs. He would promise them whatever they wanted in life. God informed the dinosaurs that the reptilian leader would promise to provide for all their needs, but he also warned that the reptilian dinosaur wouldn't keep his promises in the end times. In the end, they will suffer depopulation, famine, water shortages, and they will be punished if they do not comply.

He firmly stated that the reptilian dinosaur intended to gain power and control over the Judeo-Christian Dinosaur Nation through deception and concealment of the truth and he would be protected by secret anti-Judeo-Christian dinosaurs who didn't believe in freedom, liberty, or God. He warned that the reptilian false prophet would set up a myriad of charitable organizations. In fact, God warned the dinosaurs that the reptilian dinosaur would form a secret civilian army of reptilian dinosaurs who marched to his drum beat and that they would be placed in positions of power throughout the Judeo-Christian Dinosaur Nation. So, the Judeo-Christian Dinosaur Nation informed the "Minute-Dino-men" and they volunteered to guard the borders.

Unfortunately, because the Judeo-Christian dinosaurs never had to worry about their leaders protecting their nation, the dinosaurs let their guard down.

They were too trusting. After all, Judeo-Christian dinosaurs felt safe and they became a nation of passive citizens. They didn't bother to learn anything about politics. They didn't attend meetings. They didn't question their leaders. In fact, the dinosaurs didn't have any major problems with their leaders in the past and didn't pay much attention to the warnings by the Elder dinosaurs, so they were easy prey by their hunters. The dinosaur citizens lived fearless lives and their nation was known as the super powerful on earth. Their former dinosaur leaders weren't perfect, but for the most part, they had been trustworthy in the past.

The wise spiritual elder of the Dinosaur Nation, Dinomoses #I, had been elected to lead the Dinosaur Nation. The majority of dinosaurs sought the advice of Dinomoses and he believed that he was called by God to climb to the top of the nearby mountain for an important message to be handed down to the Dinosaur Nation's citizens. Dinomoses obeyed God's command and on the Judeo-Christian day of prayer, Dinomoses followed God's instructions. Dinomoses was a great King of the Dinosaur Nation, but he didn't dress like royalty and instead, he dressed in simple clothing and refused to wear a crown on his head. He wore a long thin gray robe and a pair of thin sole leather sandals on his worn flat feet. He carried a long thick rod made from the limb of a tree for leverage to help him hike up to the top of the mountain. Once he reached the top of the mountain, he looked around, but he didn't see anything or hear anything. He did as instructed and built an altar. He built ten pillars. He burned incense. And, he sacrificed an ox.

The hours passed and Dinomoses didn't hear anything from God. The air was still, but he did feel the warm winds whistle through the skies and he felt the winds gently blowing against his deeply wrinkled face. Dinomoses looked up towards the sky in confusion and prayed, "Lord, where are you?" Dinomoses wasn't getting any answers and he began doubting himself.

Suddenly, a gust of strong wind blew across the mountain and knocked Dinomoses to his knees. His long white beard and long white wiry hair blew in the wind. He closed his twinkling blue eyes to avoid the dust and fervently prayed and repented from his sins. Suddenly, the warmth from a burning bush covered with golden flames appeared before him. He heard the noises. Crackle. Crackle. Crackle. In an instant, the skies grew dark with grayness all about.

Thunder roared. Lightning struck. Dinomoses was overwhelmed by the sudden storm.

At that moment, he heard a strong firm voice that said, "Dinomoses, 'I am the Lord your God. I have chosen you to take the Tablet embedded on this mountainside to my followers. I shall carve the Ten Commandments in stone with my finger and the Judeo-Christian Dinosaur Nation that I created and Blessed must obey these simple moral laws or else they will suffer and create a nation of chaos, crisis, death, illness, and greed if they sell out to the material world. God told Dinomoses, "I have blessed you and that is why you are healthy and have lived a long life upon the earth. You and your sons were chosen to lead the Judeo-Christian Nation."

God said "Rise up, Dinomoses. Remove the Ten Commandments etched in stone from the mountain side and take the Tablet back to the dinosaur nation and instruct them to follow my commandments."

The storm stopped. Dinomoses opened his eyes. He witnessed the sunrise.

The sun's golden glow encircled it. As Dinomoses felt the warmth from the sun, a feeling of peace came over Dinomoses. He felt empowered and energized and renewed. His eyes filled with tears as he grabbed onto his stick and stood up. He looked up to the heavens and said, "Thank You, Lord, I am not worthy of such an honor, but I shall obey." Dinomoses walked over to the mountainside and carefully removed The Commandments which he intended to carry back to the Judeo-Christian Nation. He couldn't wait to share the good news.

Dinomoses felt blessed to be chosen for this task. He was filled with joy. His walk down the side of the mountain allowed him to recall what he had just experienced. He felt overwhelmed with happiness. He felt anxious as he walked back down the rocky trail and towards the Dinosaur Nation, although he did feel somewhat disoriented as if he had awakened from a glorious dream. He was reassured that he wasn't dreaming because he had the physical Ten Commandment Tablet in his hand. These would be the supreme laws of the land for the Judeo-Christian Nation that would create a civilized nation so they could live in harmony upon the earth with God's creations as well as Mother Nature and each other.

Dinomoses felt blessed by his experience and he couldn't wait to tell the Judeo-Christian dinosaurs about his experiences on the mountain top. He hurried to greet the other dinosaurs. As he neared the village, Dinomoses stopped in his tracks. He was shocked. He stared straight ahead at his Dinosaur Nation. His shock turned to anger. He stopped and stared.

The dinosaurs were partying. They were performing lustful sexual acts and sinful acts. He couldn't believe that they had built a golden idol and that they were dancing around the golden idol and worshipping the golden dinosaur idol. They were filled with drunkenness and lust. The first commandment on the Tablets etched in stone by God read that they were not to worship false gods or false idols before God.

Dinomoses was ashamed of his fellow dinosaurs. The anger he experienced ran through his veins felt like burning flames. Tears flowed from his eyes and down his cheeks.

His voice roared like a lion, "Stop! Stop! Stop worshipping that false idol!"

Dinomoses was so distraught. He struck his stick against a rock that caused a lightning bolt and caught their attention. He angrily shouted, "Listen to me! You have sinned against God. You have angered God!" His voice rang out like thunder and frightened the dinosaurs.

Dinomoses couldn't suppress his anger. He lifted the Tablet above his head that laid out the dinosaur's Ten Commandments carved into stone and thrust it to the ground. The dinosaur Tablet broke in half and he left it lying on the ground. The dinosaurs stopped their immoral behaviors and worshipping the false idol and became silent. They stood still and they felt ashamed of their actions as they realized they had brought shame upon their village and disrespected themselves and the Elders and fell out of favor with God.

At that very moment, roaring thunder shook the ground and lightening bolts struck the earth. The skies were black and dismal. Heavy rain began to pour down and large balls of hail fell upon them as they sought shelter. The hail crashed against the golden idol that they had secretly built. Sadly, the secret atheists in the village had been influencing many of the young dinosaurs and led them astray and away. They led them away from God and morality which is how Dino and Dina were thrown out of God's Sacred Garden and forced to be tested upon the earth by their future works and prayers and repentance and used to spread God's message to future dinosaurs and species.

The atheists convinced many of the youth that God didn't exist. They led them to believe that their parents were "old school" and that they could do anything they desired without fear of punishment. They taught them that there were no consequences to their actions.

Dinomoses looked up and shouted, "You have offended God. These are God's tears falling down upon us!" The dinosaurs looked up at the skies. The white clouds turned an eerie gray. Roaring thunder and lightning struck! Fear filled their minds. Dinomoses shouted at the dinosaurs, "Destroy the golden idol, or the Judeo-Christian Dinosaur Nation shall be destroyed. You have been warned!"

Dinomoses shook his head and he cried out, "What have you done?" He couldn't believe what he witnessed after he had experienced being so close to God.

"Repent from your sins and ask for forgiveness!" he demanded. At that exact moment. The ground began to move and shake. The dinosaurs cried out for God's mercy. Dinomoses didn't feel the earthquake as he walked to his cave. He didn't seem to notice the rumbling upon the earth's surface. He felt nothing but shame as tears flowed from his eyes.

A few days later, the rain stopped. The dinosaur citizens felt remorseful throughout the nation. The Judeo-Christian dinosaurs felt ashamed as they worked hard to destroy the golden idol. Afterwards, the dinosaur Tablet that listed the dinosaur's Ten Commandments became the law of the land. In fact, after Dinomoses prayed for forgiveness and asked for God's mercy as he walked about the Dinosaur Nation. Suddenly he stopped. He noticed that the dinosaur Tablet had been miraculously restored. He picked up the dinosaur's Tablet and looked up and said, "Thank you, Lord. Thank you for sparing our nation." After the dust settled, the dinosaurs built a special altar made of gold and silver and they carefully placed the dinosaur's Ten Commandments securely inside so that they would be protected and untouched by anyone else.

The dinosaur's elected elders created new dino-made laws as the dinosaur population continued to increase. Freedom and Liberty were upheld. Welfare and Safety of the Judeo-Christian dinosaur citizens was established. These established laws would secure the borders. But, as the population of dinosaurs increased, the younger dinosaurs split off and created new groups such as the radicals, liberals, feminists, conservatives, independents, and moral majority. Eventually, Dinomoses #I, passed away as well as, Dinomoses #II. Dinomoses # III carried on with the tradition of leading the Dinosaurs in the right direction.

Noah spent hours decoding the Tablets without a break because he was so fascinated with the legend when he suddenly realized that he was hungry, so he snacked on a protein bar and poured a cup of coffee and grabbed a ripe mango. He realized that everything the dinosaurs ate or drank was organic and contained the maximum amount of natural vitamins and minerals that created strong immune systems. Noah believed that God created oxygen and the immune system to protect all species so their bodies and minds could naturally fight off viruses and germs. The truth is that all species carry germs, viruses and bacteria inside their bodies from the time a baby is born. He chuckled, if God hadn't invented the immune system and all the foods and herbs and plants that contain vitamins, minerals, and amino acids protein, and oxygen, no species would have survived.

The genius of God's creation of human DNA, oxygen and water supplies needed for life and healthy immune systems amazed Noah. After all, these necessities of life effect the insects, fish, plants, trees, and all living creatures upon the earth amazed Noah. The thought of how today's modern world was destroying the environment concerned Noah. He continued to write notes in his journal and included that it's human beings that are responsible for creating harmful chemicals and bioweapons or foods. It is humans who contaminated the air, soil and waters destroying the eco-system and these same wealthy NWO corporate CEO's who stripped the environment of its natural habitats and growth for-profit. They've turned against the Middle Class workers and decided to blame the Middle Class and indigent in order to justify their goal of reducing the population under the guise of saving the planet.

They seek to wipe out all that God created upon the earth. It appears that it has always been a battle involving the Survival of the Fittest for all species since time began. I thought it was good to live passively, but now I realize that living passive lifestyles and ignoring the dangers created by evil ones may be part of the downfall of all species since time began as nothing remains the same while good people remain complicit and ignore the truth. Time doesn't stand still nor does change. It appears that evil people never sleep.

Noah thought about the water that he was drinking and brought him back to current times in the USA. In the jungle he was drinking crystal clear water that was untouched by wealthy men and women seeking to control the water supply in the USA and around the world. Noah believed that most people didn't think about it or realize what was happening to the oceans, rivers, lakes, air supply and soil as the industrial age expanded and globalized. They didn't realize they were creating garbage island by throwing their plastic trash into the oceans while boating that caused the fish and animals and plant life to die or maybe, they didn't care. He took another sip of refreshing pure sweet spring water. As a kid, he remembered when he and his friends gathered in the summer or after school and drank right out of the hose without getting sick every day. No one ever got sick from drinking from the hose, but don't dare do it today.

Noah believed that the government of each state and the federal government led the American people to believe that their water supplies were safe, but if that was true then why did they add Fluoride to the water and the toothpaste and lie about it as a benefit? He remembered how the oil companies got approval from the EPA to dump MTBE toxic poison into the gas tanks that were carcinogenic and leaked into the drinking water supplies and soil until it was exposed after many people were diagnosed with cancer in certain cities.

CHAPTER 6

Sheriff Joe's in Town

As time passed and progressed into more modern days for the Judeo-Christian Dinosaur Nation, the Judeo-Christian dinosaurs elected Sheriff Dinojoe to head up the army of Minute Dinomen who volunteered to protect their borders and uphold their laws. But, since their Judeo-Christian Dinosaur Nation had little incident of crimes or foreign immigration, the natural-born dinosaurs became even more passive and careless about their borders.

Sometimes, the volunteers would sit around and play cards or drink coffee and eat dino-doughnuts. Sheriff Dinojoe was serious about his job. He wasn't a slacker and always feared that there was always a possibility of other species who may seek to invade the Judeo-Christian Dinosaur Nation and harm them. He always thought there was a possibility that one day foreign enemies would attempt to steal their homeland from them. He didn't believe in being passive or careless when it came to secured borders as a matter of safety and precaution.

Of course, a group of young dinosaurs were seeking to be independent of the Elders and their parents. They felt it was time to change their lifestyle from what they believed were outdated old fashion traditions and rules. The dinosaur youth respected Sheriff Dinojoe and Officer Dinomack and they looked up to them. If the young dinosaurs spotted Sheriff Dinojoe or Officer Dinomack, they would ask them to sit with them under a Weeping Willow tree and share their adventures when they had to face danger.

The young dinosaurs and even adults would anxiously await the wonderful stories of how The Sheriff and Officer Dinomack caught the bad dinosaurs, but they wanted to know what happens inside the Femasaurus camps and if the rumors that dinosaurs could be reprogrammed if they didn't obey and comply?

Of course, Sheriff Dinojoe and Officer Dinomack loved to mingle with the youth. Officer Dinomack couldn't resist a captivated audience, so they would share some of the stories with the young dinosaurs and hope that they could help them make the right choices while they were growing up. The young dinosaurs would sit quietly and listen intently as they used their imaginations.

The officers embellished their stories somewhat to keep the audience interested and on edge.

Sheriff Dinojoe and his posse stayed in touch with Officer Dino-Mack as they attempted to uphold the Rule of Law established by the Elders. Sheriff Dinojoe didn't tolerate any dinosaur who intentionally violated their laws, but the young activist dinosaurs opposed his punishments and they protested against his policies. For example, Dinojoc would tie a pink ribbon around an arrested male dinosaur's neck and tie it in a bow as part of their punishment, but the young activists felt that he was politically incorrect. Of course, Sheriff Dinojoe wouldn't back down and stuck to his guns so that those who took the wrong path would think twice and get back on track.

A STRANGER IN TOWN

One day, an unexpected stranger slipped into the Dinosaur Nation without being identified by the Minute-Dino-men. The stranger suddenly appeared in the Dinosaur Nation as if he arrived on a magic carpet from across the oceans. He appeared confident, youthful, and charming, but different. The citizens residing in the Dinosaur Nation never asked him, "Who are you?" In fact, no one bothered to vet him, but passively accepted his arrival. When they asked his name, the stranger would joke and say, "I'm Dinobari."

The ladies said, "He's so handsome." They liked his long sleek neck and his dark bedroom eyes that flashed his long curly lashes. His top lip formed two perfect mounts. He had a magnificent smile with bright white teeth. His chiseled jaw was perfectly formed. The stranger's light chocolate color skin set him apart from the Judeo-Christian light to medium dinosaurs.

Most of the natural-born Judeo-Christian dinosaurs had light to medium skin; however due to climate changes, there were more younger dinosaurs born with a variation of skin color and the dinosaurs nicknamed their nation, a melting pot. Nonetheless, the Judeo-Christian natural-born citizens inherited their Birthright from 2 natural-born heterosexual parents born on the soil of the Judeo-Christian Dinosaur Nation.

The young dinosaurs weren't as concerned about the color of skin that appeared to be changing because they were more accepting of change and of dinosaurs that didn't all meet the stereotype in appearance of what the Elders believed were the super powerful race of dinosaurs. The controversy was created because the youth believed that there were places that were extremely hot or extremely cold with little sunshine that cause the changes of the dinosaur's skin color. They didn't believe they could be the only dinosaurs walking upon the earth.

But, the unidentified dark skin dinosaur, a stranger in the Judeo-Christian Dinosaur Nation, remained a mystery. Yet, he appeared confident, intelligent, and likable. It was obvious that the female dinosaurs were smitten with him. In fact, he encouraged young female dinosaurs to demand the right to abort unborn Judeo-Christian dinosaurs. This shocked the Elders and called it immoral.

They noted that the magnificent stranger in town liked to party. Dance, Socialize. He wandered into the local pub for a cold beer and greeted Sheriff Dinojoe who was curious to find out more about Dinobari. In fact, the Elders asked Sheriff Dinojoe if they could find out where Dinobari was born and where was his Homeland or why did he decide to enter into the Judeo-Christian Dinosaur Nation.

Dinobari at the Pub

The unidentified magnificent dinosaur trotted like a race horse through the village. He appeared friendly and confident. Dinomoses the III watched him strutting his long legs through the streets as if he had important places to go. Dinomoses had a flash back and he remembered his great grandfather telling him the story about the golden idol. He thought that the stranger resembled the golden idol described by his grandpa which stirred his curiosity even more. "I don't know why, but I don't trust the new stranger in town, Dinobari," remarked Dinomoses.

The younger dinosaurs scoffed at the Elder's comments. After all, the youth welcomed change. A young outspoken dinosaur who wanted to be one of the future leaders, Dinocary, was standing nearby.

The young dinosaur, Dinocarney, exuded an air of arrogance. He smirked and boldly said, "You're just getting old, gramps." He paused and said, "You are old school and we're new school. Your ideas are outdated. Besides, Dinobari is cool! Dinobari believes he could bring change and transformation to the Judeo-Christian Dinosaur Nation."

Dinomoses just shook his head. He felt as if everything the Elders established was being shredded because the youth don't get how important established laws, traditions, and morality help to maintain and mold a nation.

Dinocarney stated, "I wonder where he got those sunglasses. I'd sure like to have a pair." He paused and remarked, "Besides, Dinobari likes to play basketball and the dinosaur kids can't wait to challenge him to a game."

Dinobari playing basketball

Dinomoses scratched his head. He decided to lay down under a fully shaded Elm tree that lined one street. He stared at the new stranger in town and watched him meet up with some of the female dinosaurs who were swooning over him while he played a game of basketball with the male dinosaurs. Dinahillary, Dinanancy, and Dinasusan were definitely infatuated with him. It appeared that the young female dinosaurs didn't care about the rumor that Dinobari's dad was married with dinosaur kids when his light skin dinosaur mom conceived him and gave birth or that his paternal grandma stated he was born in Kenyaville.

A few minutes later, the new stud in town excused himself to meet up with some of the more questionable characters in town who were powerful and very wealthy bankers. Dinomoses noticed that Obamasaurus, which Dinomoses believed was his real name was confused as to why he introduced himself as Dinobari to the youth, but when speaking with key members of the nation, he was Obamasaurus which surprised Dinomoses. He wondered why he would be meeting with Dinogeorge, Dinohenry, and Dinobill (nicknamed slick Billy) and Dinogaites. These same wealthy elitist dinosaurs conspired to overthrow Dinomoses III as the generational leader of the Judeo-Christian Dinosaur Nation and that worried Dinomoses. The Liberal Socialist dinosaurs were conspiring to bring in a more youthful leader. In fact, Dinomoses feared that they were conspiring with the radical dinosaurs, but that was only a rumor that had been floating around amongst the Elders.

Sometimes, Dinomoses felt as if Obamasaurus aka Dinobari was up to no good, but he couldn't quite put his finger on it. The new stranger in town stood tall. He held his head up high. His smile revealed an air of arrogance all about him. Sometimes, he would close his eyes as if he was meditating or praying.

Dinomoses grumbled, "I bet the stranger in town was a spoiled child and always got his way. I don't know what it is about him, but I don't trust him." He heard rumors that his dad was a dark radical who resented the light to medium dinosaurs of the Judeo-Christian Dinosaur faith and favored a radical political and religious belief that was in opposition to the Judeo-Christian Dinosaur laws, religion, and way of life, but he didn't know if the rumors were true or false.

However, a majority of the Judeo-Christian dinosaurs bought into the radical agenda that dinosaurs need to be tolerant of the stranger in town even if he refused to identify himself to Sheriff Dinojoe. They began labeling dinosaurs as racists if they questioned the new stranger in town, The more youthful dinosaur activists defended tolerance and political correctness. They liked the buzz words, i.e., hope, change, transformation, forward, progress, collectivism, socialism, communism, even though they didn't even know the name of the Mayor of the Judeo-Christian Dinosaur Nation or that a stranger in town and his supporters present their ideas as cool and exciting and progressive, but could bring crisis and devastation to the Judeo-Christian Nation by being passive.

Nonetheless, the busy dinosaurs went about their daily chores. The mommy dinosaurs prepared dinner for their families while the daddy dinosaurs spent their day hunting for food and water. The male dinosaurs worked hard to make sure there was more than a 90-day supply of emergency food and water stored in their kitchen cupboards. The dinosaurs were an intelligent species and they understood that climate change could bring about drought and famine. Climate change could also bring about snow storms, hurricanes, tsunamis, tornadoes, earthquakes, wildfires, or floods. Any of these natural disasters threatened the survival of the dinosaurs as well as their homes, water and food supplies needed for the animals dependent on a balanced environment. The dinosaurs grew vegetables and fruits and herbs on their private properties. They saved rainwater. They realized that life was about the survival of the fittest which included the ants and squirrels who worked hard during the summer to store up for the long winter months and for their survival.

The Judeo-Christian pro-life civilization increased in population as commanded by God. The married youth continued to marry and give birth to large families of dinosaur babies who would grow up and continue to preserve their race and their nation in the future.

The majority of new dinosaur moms breast fed their baby dinosaurs and the baby dinosaurs thrived. The dinosaur dads were protective of their families as God commanded them to do. They provided for their families and in exchange, the wife and dino-kids loved their dino-dad. They believed that procreation was a natural part of God's plan to fill the earth with living species and keep life upon the earth moving forward from generation to generation as long as the Judeo-Christian nations didn't turn their backs on the Judeo-Christian God and Ten Commandments.

The Judeo-Christian dinosaurs instinctively understood that traditional marriage preserved the dinosaur species so the natural born citizens of the Judeo-Christian dinosaur nation could continue to preserve the laws, roots, traditions, and culture of their nation for future generations. They understood the importance of the traditional family.

Dinomoses always said, "The family is the foundation of a civilized Judeo-Christian Dinosaur Nation. If the traditional family unit is destroyed by secret societies then we will see civil unrest in our nation and we will become uncivilized."

In fact, the Elders encouraged the youth in every village to volunteer for the dinosaur's Boy Scout troops, but Dinobari required that the dinosaur kids sign up for what he called the Dinosaur National Civilian Security Force, (DNCSF). The majority of dinosaur parents didn't have a clue what he was talking about at the time. Dinobari mentioned that the DNCSF would be more powerful and more well-funded than the dinosaur's national military army.

The statements made by the stranger in town upset the elders. The youth had been trained to guard the borders and to march along the borders holding a red, white and blue flag with stars and stripes. In fact, the dinosaur's Rules of Law granted all dinosaurs the right to bear arms. So, the troops would voluntarily carve spears as their weapons for protection. They also had the right to defend themselves and their families.

The dinosaur conservatives were strict constitutionalists and believed in following the Rule of Law without exception. The dino-youth were eager to change their nation because they were enamored with Dinobari and his recruitment of young dinos into his Civilian National Security Force which the Elders opposed.

CHAPTER 7

Change and Transformation: Officer Dinomack

The Judeo-Christian dinosaurs weren't happy with the idea of their leaders using their dino-kids to learn how to march to the drum beat of the secret society's army who carry weapons. They wanted their Judeo-Christian Dinosaur Nation to remain peaceful and free and liberated. They also didn't like their leaders trampling on the dinosaurs' parental rights and making decisions and choices for dinosaur kids. This became a controversial topic amongst the parents and the Elders.

After taking a break, Noah continued to read the Tablets that revealed a more passive nation of dinosaur citizens. They wanted to believe that their leaders protected the welfare and safety of every dinosaur citizen. He read that in the early mornings, the mommy dinosaurs strolled through the neighborhoods with their dinosaur kids until they reached the swimming pool of water. The kids splashed in the cold water on warm sunny days and were quite playful being around other dino-kids.

Noah thought, at least the Judeo-Christian moral dinosaurs didn't have to worry about excessive government regulations. The dinosaurs had freedoms guaranteed to them by their Judeo-Christian God which was carved into the dinosaur Tablets. The dinosaur legend noted that the Elders understood that change is imminent in the world, but only if they followed the traditions, integrity, and values of their nation's established laws.

Thus, the Elders believed that the dinosaur citizens and dinosaur kids were straying away from their original traditions and embracing foreign anti-Judeo-Christian dinosaur beliefs. Dinomoses worried that too many dinosaurs had already turned away from God. He was concerned that God's wrath could include climate change as punishment. The elders believed that global warming or an Ice Age could devastate their very survival.

The Elders were aware that even a slight increase or decrease in the weather and the temperature wasn't of any concern, but any rapid changes would affect the health of the dinosaurs and the food and water supplies. Most of the citizens respected Dinomoses for his wise opinions about climate change, but he avoided causing fear and emotional distress.

Dinomoses told Officer Dinomack, "We've always feared that there was a possibility of global warming or an Ice Age, but I don't think we're even close to reaching those dangerous weather conditions and temperatures, so everyone should just go about their business. It wouldn't hurt for you and Sheriff Dinojoe to hold Town Hall meetings with the villagers and suggest they prepare for either. We could suggest that they create a business that they might call "Dino-Preppers."

Noah believed that the dinosaurs didn't have a clue that one day the dinosaurs living in the Judeo-Christian Dinosaur Nation would roam the earth as a powerful species and worry about facing climate changes that could rock their world. He whispered to himself, "Even our nation didn't anticipate that the American voters would preselect and elect unidentified public servants to high positions of power, slip them into office and not once, but 3 times!"

In a near trans like moment, he paused and mumbled, "So, I doubt that the majority of dinosaurs could imagine that one day an unidentified non-believer would end up as the leader of the Judeo-Christian Dinosaur Nation." Noah remembered when the new unidentified U.S. President stated, "I will skyrocket electricity and bankrupt the coal mining states." He also mocked Jesus Christ and the Sermon on the Mount and the Bible" and yet he was re-elected.

Of course, Noah realized that all living species and environmental trees and plants, water and oxygen have a common thread. Every living creation upon the earth uses their instinct to survive upon the earth and must remain vigilant against any creature who destroys healthy trees, plants, soil, water, oxygen and life. It is a world that demands the "survival of the fittest" in mind, body and spirit. It is human beings that haven't learned to put aside ego and greed and arrogance as the evil ones destroy the once healthy balance between God, Humanity and Mother Nature. It appears wealthy people stripped the environment based on profits and greed. They seek to play God and reduce the population of innocent people.

Noah picked up his notebook and wanted to recall his thoughts, so he wrote them down so he wouldn't forget. They felt important. Noah wrote that God's creations are constantly under attack. All creatures instinctively know that life is about the survival of the fittest. Survival and health must be nurtured just like a mother nurtures their babies and children until they can survive on their own. Yet, we see animals caring for babies and their little ones, but people ignore aborting human babies, which Noah couldn't justify in his mind.

Humans sometimes forget to be caring and share love by acts of kindness towards not only ourselves and families and friends or co-workers, but for all creatures. The environment's trees and plants, water and oxygen that keep us alive and healthy, he jotted down. The herbs provide medicinal cures and the water cleanses our bodies and refreshes us as well as moisturizes our skin. We take these things for granted but they are being polluted and adversely affect our bodies and minds until we become the endangered species in a world smothered by greed.

After a pause, Noah thought about today. It appears that mankind is self-destructive and although the unborn babies used as human commodities for profit should be on the endangered species list as #1 over the animals listed, it appears that every human being is becoming an endangered species based on greed by greedy government leaders and Wall Street investors involved with secret societies and Big Pharma. It's evil in Noah's eyes to force people to be used as human lab rats to be used for experimental chemical laden medical treatments without consent, but under duress of losing their jobs and their freedom and social life as has been proven throughout history when psychopaths take control over nations.

Noah continued his writing and wrote that millions of people who died over the years were permanently injured for life after their doctors jabbed them with FDA approved vaccines or prescribed chemical-laden drugs and used them for their experiments in secret. The media and government stated that these Rx's and vaccines were FDA approved and licensed as 100% safe for distribution, but tens of thousands of people died or were permanently injured for life. The cases filed were settled outside of a trial by high powered lawyers which led major stories turned into a few sentences and forgotten.

Noah stopped writing. He placed his pen in his shirt pocket and leaned over and dropped his journal inside his backpack. He felt as if he was being awakened from his sleep by living in the untouched environment of the jungles where there weren't any chemicals and preservatives or boxed foods, but he knew Wall Street would destroy them too, over time. Noah was a student of nutrition and concerned about how the dinosaurs remained healthy or the people in the Bible who lived for 400 years and even gave birth during their elderly years survived much longer than today's modern world who claims to have more medical science and technology to keep people alive when the average lifespan in America is 78 versus the past when dinosaurs and people were recorded to live so much longer. He believed it had to do with chemicals, preservatives, radiation, and microwaves strangling the planet.

Noah got back to work and continued to decipher the Tablets and symbols and drawings. He believed that one of the key messages left by Dinomoses for the Judeo-Christian Nations included that "The Rule of Law must include justice for all. Equality. Fairness. Morals. Principles. Integrity. Honesty. Fairness. Mercy. He even included Common Sense and the Sanctity of Life for all living species. He believed that the Rule of Law must be adhered to and enforced to maintain a civilized nation where the citizens are safe and remain free."

Dinomoses wrote that the weather affected their health, food, and water supplies. He stated, "Mother Nature can be kind to the Judeo-Christian dinosaurs and other species upon the earth, but she can also destroy the world of dinosaurs if they do not respect Mother Nature and God and all creatures living upon the earth that was created by God to be in balance with the universe and our planet."

Noah couldn't stop reading the Tablets. He was fascinated by the untold secret legend. The Tablets noted that the dinosaurs trusted everyone. Noah read the farmers provided vegetables and fruits to sell at the Farmers Market.

The farmers concerned themselves with political issues. They realized that the importance of feeding and caring for the animals that would some times suddenly appear on their land who need food and water.

One afternoon, Dinomoses made an effort to stop by and spend some time and visit with the Farmers. He wanted to know their thoughts about the food supply and the stranger in town with 2 names, Dinobari and Obamasaurus. One of the farmers who called himself, dinomike met up with Dinmoses and told him that their concerns were infrastructure which was in dire need to prevent flooding and destroying the crops or drowning the animals so they can survive as well.

Farmer dinomike, a medium-size dinosaur, but muscular from his hard work taking care of his farm. Dinomike told Dinomoses that the farmers didn't trust wealthy Dinoal who continually fear mongered over climate change and increasing taxes while he didn't contribute anything to the Judeo-Christian Nation. He appeared to be a talker and a taker, not a giver. Dinoal was a tall stocky dinosaur with round brown eyes. He spoke with a deep raspy voice who lived in a mansion that probably spanned 40,000 sq. ft and used up several lots. His mansion blocked the sunlight at times as well as the ocean view and the ocean breeze that provided fresh air and ions. The ions were known to keep the lungs and brain healthy as well as the immune system. Dinoal was constantly fear mongering about global warming and the Ice Age, but what did he ever say that would prevent the earth from reacting to unknown events?

Dinoal approached Dinomoses and said, "You know we're concerned about climate change one day destroying the earth. The sun's temperature is rising at such high levels that they could destroy the crops. The plants and the trees are rotting. The heat is drying up the soil. The food supplies are being diminished.

We should fear more droughts. We don't know what to do. I think we need to demand that the dinosaurs turn over more of their food and water supplies to me and my wealthy dinosaur partners for storage and redistribution. There are storage units built under the ground for surplus food and water supplies."

Dinomoses wasn't fond of Dinoal and he replied in a loud voice, "Don't worry. Pray for God's blessings. The underground storage won't help if Mother Nature buries the earth in ice or drought. We'll just be taken to meet our Maker." Dinomoses was aware of the weather changing which Dinoal referred to as Climate Change and global warming. He didn't trust Dinoal and his wealthy dinosaur partners who he believed were anti-Judeo-Christians and didn't believe in a Higher Power because they were so wealthy that they believed they were the higher power upon the earth who could control the weather, food, water, and the nation.

In another part of the Tablet, it mentioned that a popular Judeo-Christian Pastor, Dinorick, shopped at the Farmers Market and stopped by. Pastor Dinorick was wealthy and he had a substantial following and a large dino-cave church. He even provided free dino-doughnuts. Pastor Dinorick approached Dinomoses. Pastor Dinorick stated, "I met with the magnificent stranger in town, Obamasaurus. He and I should incorporate all foreign religions into my church and create a one world religion. After all, a substantial number of dinosaurs are slacking off in attendance at church, especially the youth. Many dino-kids aren't showing up for Sunday School and that is a serious concern for the church and for their parents."

Dinomoses felt anger racing through his veins. He replied, "I've noticed that traditional marriage is declining among the young people and the radical dinosaurs are promoting same-sex marriages which would reduce the population of the Judeo-Christians because same-sex couples can't procreate, so what about that? Pastor Dinorick was speechless and said, "Yes, we'll have to consider that in the future. Have a blessed day, Dinomoses.," as he walked away.

A few days later, Sheriff, Dinojoe, shouted out, "Hear ye! Hear ye! All dinosaurs are ordered to attend a Town Hall Meeting in the center of the Dinosaur Nation after dinner tonight." He posted the message carved in stone in various places so everyone would show up at the meeting. So, after the sun went down, the dinosaurs curiously scurried into the center of the village for a Town Hall meeting. The audience anxiously waited for the meeting to start.

They were curious to learn why the mayor, Dinorahm, insisted on a Town Hall Meeting on short notice. The dinosaurs waited patiently. They couldn't wait to hear what was so urgent.

Dinomoses walked up to the center of the stage and looked around at the audience. He breathed deeply and stated, "I called everyone here tonight to inform you that the Dinosaur Nation could be on the verge of global warming.

The dinosaurs sighed with fear. Silence fell across the audience. He said, "I'm not saying it will happen, but I think we need to double down on our emergency supplies. This statement shocked the dinosaurs in the audience.

They gasped. Silence fell upon the entire audience, but they agreed.

Although, every dinosaur was excited about the issues that their leaders presented to them, they realized that stocking up for emergencies was a good idea and agreed with Dimomoses. No one can predict the weather. Dinomoses and his generational family had been their leaders for generations and they didn't have any intention of voting in a new leader when the elections approached.

But, as time passes by and new generations grow up, a generation of youth who were of voting age didn't hold back that they were ready for change and that they were open to new leaders running for office.

The Elders believed that hope and change wasn't a good thing because they were wise men who questioned change. They knew that the grass wasn't always greener on the other side and it could lead to serious problems. They believed that traditions and beliefs rooted into a Judeo-Christian foundation led to a civilized free nation. They also knew that change introduced by foreigners could undermine a strong Judeo-Christian foundation to rise and fall if they weren't careful. The youth were warned as well as the elders, parents and grandparents that evil can seduce a nation and blind them to the truth. As usual, young dinosaurs don't pay much attention. The times were changing as the leaders became elderly.

Therefore, the Elders of the Judeo-Christian nation including the respected Sheriff DinoJoe, and Officer DinoMack, who were not buying into hope and change or transforming their nation into a foreign nation could see a potential crisis coming on the horizon and it was a can of worms that could never be closed if it was opened.

The Elders believed any changes to their existing laws posed a grave threat to the unsuspecting good dinosaur citizens. After all, the Judeo-Christian laws were carved in stone by God since the Judeo-Christian Nation had been established. They realized that foreign laws would wipe out their existing laws should a foreign enemy seduce the dinosaurs by grooming a youthful dinosaur exuding charisma. Energy. A New Face on the block. Excitement of a stranger appearing on the scene. His cool designer sunglasses were a hit. The Elders feared that their existence and history could be wiped out and erased and forgotten forever from the entire universe; however, the young dino-kids didn't feel the same way. In fact, they enjoyed biking with Dinobari who the Elders called Obamasaurus.

Dinobari showing off on the latest Dino-Bike

Although Noah was tired, he continued deciphering the codes carved into the Tablets. The Tablets revealed that the dinosaurs were innovative and creative and many appeared to be mechanically inclined. He was impressed and he couldn't believe his eyes. He saw a carving of Dinobari riding on a dino-bike that the dinosaurs manufactured by hand with rocks, wood, metal, and other materials they dug out of the ground or picked up in the caves.

Noah was fascinated with the drawings of the dinosaurs warming themselves around a fireside which made him believe that they figured out how to create a fire from dry wood and stay warm in the winters. He was surprised that they invented so many weapons and were prepared to defend themselves from foreign enemies. The dinosaur citizens established the right to bear arms and form a civilian army. Noah chuckled as he spotted a carved picture of Obamasuarus with his thumbs up wearing his designer dino-sunglasses. Noah laughed. He said, "Dinobari or Obamsaurus truly is a Rock Star." Maybe, he missed his true calling. He had plenty of fans.

The fact that Obamasaurus had so many talents was a mystery to many dinosaurs. The male-dinosaurs would get together and chat. They wondered where did he learn so much about sports and travel they pondered. He rarely mentioned his mother and a father or his grandparents. In fact, he didn't say much about his friends or his past as if he was concealing it and he had something to hide. He mentioned that he was educated. The Elders felt that Obamasaurus also known as Dinobari was hiding something from them, but they just didn't know what it might be. They were determined to find out.

Dinobari enjoyed competing in track. He enjoyed sports so his flexible lifestyle made him even more interesting to the dino-citizens. These were the things that made him popular with the dino-youth and young adults. The Elders couldn't run track or ride a bike any longer or play basketball. It appeared he had it all. And, he could sing and dance. The Elders didn't know how to compete with all his talents which gave Dinobari an advantage. He shared his liberal ideas with the dino-youth and made it even more difficult to convince the dino-kids that traditions are important.

The dinosaurs were fascinated with Dinobari. It appeared that he could join them on track and run for charitable causes such as helping the schools earn more money for their school supplies and field trips. He even promised to remodel the gym and build a weight room so the athletes could maintain their weight and strength while competing in sports. Dinobari's mind was filled with promises and hope. The dino-youth were sold on his ideas and changes that he stated he would bring to their Judeo-Christian Dinosaur Nation. He brought energy and sparked the interests of the wealthy business owners, not just the youth.

Dinobari Running Track

CHAPTER 8

The Town Hall Meeting

During the next Town Hall meeting the following week called to order by the Mayor Dinorahm. The Mayor took the mic and introduced himself and said, "We have a new dino-lawyer in town. He believes that he has the solutions to preserve our Judeo-Christian Dinosaur Nation. He praised him as a prominent and well-respected dino-lawyer and a dino-Professor of Law at a prominent University of Law. Mayor Dinorahm invited him to stand up. He did and then sat back down.

Mayor Dinorham said, "He believes he can bring hope and change to our Dinosaur Judeo-Christian Nation and transform it over the next four years. He believes that he's the one." Sitting on stage with the Mayor were wealthy bankers and businessmen who donated to the Obamasuaurus campaign for president. Dinowilly. Dinogeorge. Dinoal. Dinojesse. Dinohenry. Dinojb. The Mayor said, Obamasaurus will say a few words, so let's welcome him to come up to the stage.

The mysterious stranger with his long neck holding his head up high trotted across the stage wearing his cool dark designer dino-sunglasses. The young girls were impressed. His ears perked up and out. He stood in the center of the stage and held onto the microphone and the written speech. He smiled. He looked around at the audience. His glistening pectorals made the female dinosaurs swoon. He began his 'Chicken Little' speech. He said, "Dinosaurs of the world, I've come to the Dinosaur Nation to bring transformation to your nation and move your Dinosaur Nation forward. I am a Citizen of the Dinosaur World. I use the reptilian side of my brain to make important decisions. I will take care of all your necessities of life. Trust me. The only people who you can't trust are dinosaurs who don't tell the truth because they have something to hide." Dinabarbara hosts a popular televisaurus talk show that many dinosaurs watch everyday. She interviewed Obamasaurus on her daily show and he was a hit guest with the audience.

The next day, after Obamasaurus appeared on her show, the show proved the power of the media once the audience got a good view of Obamasaurus.

The females were sold. His dino-wife, Dinomikel, spoke of Obamasaurus' home country of Kenyaville, which was across the oceans. Obamasaurus spoke of his foreign-born dark dinosaur grandma who lived in Kenyaville. His grandma stated in a media interview that Obamasaurus was born in Kenyaville and she was present at the hospital when he was born to his light skin dinosaur mother from a distant nation; however, not one dino-reporter questioned that Dinobari or Obamasaurus was not eligible to be President of the Judeo-Christian Dinosaur Nation because he was foreign-born as well as his dad so he should be disqualified, but it appeared the dice were cast and the money was donated and the cards were stacked against Dinomoses and the Elders and the Judeo-Christian Dinosaur nation.

The talk show hosts invited Mrs. Obamasaurus to appear on their late night talk shows as well, especially Dinodavid, who loved the new stranger in town. Obamasaurus told the audience that his real father was foreign-born in Kenyaville and that they believed that the Judeo-Christian Dinosaur Nation was oppressive. He said that their family believed that the Judeo-Christian dinosaurs were spoiled and prejudice, so he wanted to change and transform their behaviors and then he laughed. The audience thought he was joking. The audience laughed. They applauded. Dinodavid laughed thinking it was a joke.

The hosts on the televisaurus reported that Mrs. Obamasaurus was looking forward to vacationing and shopping abroad. His two dinosaur kids were charming. They won the hearts of the majority of dinosaur citizens. The Judeo-Christian dinosaurs appeared to be hypnotized by their words back in 2008 B.C. when the dinosaur nation was doing just fine.

Obamasaurus commented in his speech, "I don't have a lot of experience to be a leader of the Judeo-Christian Dinosaur Nation, but I promise to redistribute the Dinosaur Nation's wealth so that everyone, not just the Judeo-Christian dinosaur citizens can live a better lifestyle. I will make sure that the citizens around the world live in a better lifestyle.

He assured the Judeo-Christian dinosaurs that the members of the U.N. aka United Nomads will be given an equal redistribution of their food, water and health and housing; however no one questioned how would that be possible since the Nomads lived across the oceans. But what did the change and transformation mean? He intended to migrate the foreigners from across the oceans to set up no-go zones and take control of cities on their Homeland.

Obamasaurus and his top executive, Dinojb promised 350,000 shovel ready infrastructure jobs for the Judeo-Christian dino-workers. He promised they would build bridges across villages and roads and shelter. They would build walls to stop mudslides and protect them from ice in the winter and build dino-made pools of water to stay cool in the summer. The Judeo-Christian Dinosaur Nation bought the snake oil they sold to them, but they lied. They didn't have 350,000 shovel-ready jobs. They didn't plan on repairing and building the infrastructure or be given any housing. I'll provide thousands of shovel-ready infrastructure jobs so the dinosaurs could build dinosaur bridges and roads. After all, a female dinosaur once said that it takes a village to build a bridge.

In fact, Obamasaurus appeared on the televisaurus and stated, "My goal is to disarm the Judeo-Christian Dinosaur Nation so that all people comply with the changes that will be coming to the dinosaur nation."

The dinosaurs applauded and didn't bother to listen to what he said. He mesmerized them.

The majority of dinosaur citizens chanted, "Yes, he can!" But, they never bothered to ask, "Yes, he can do what?" Surprisingly, the dinosaur citizens or dinosaur leaders never asked, "Who are you?" In fact, tears flowed from the eyes of top celebrities such as Dinojesse and Dinoal, Dinaopra, and so many more. They were thrilled when the reaction to his popularity turned in his favor.

The unidentified stranger, Obamasaurus, believed that he could win the race against the Elder candidate, Dinocane and his running mate, Dinasarah after Dinomoses decided he wouldn't run in the race. He decided to retire. He realized that the youth were now the majority of voters and that they made up their minds. It was fairly obvious that the young voters chose to campaign for the stranger in town.

The dinosaurs were ripe for hope and change and many dinosaurs actually believed him when Obamasaurus declared during a speech that he was the messiah. In fact, his followers built a church named after him and they would pray to him in secret. They believed him when he said he could walk on water. Some dinosaurs even worshipped him and sang praises to him. They behaved as if they had been indoctrinated into a cult even though they didn't know anything about him other than what the dino-media reported. As dinoglenn stated on his televisaurus show, the Judeo-Christian dinosaur voters believed the fairy tales. His followers were acting as sheeple and they appeared to believe everything the dino-media reported about him without questioning anything.

Obamasaurus. made many promises that he didn't intend to keep, but that is politics! He promised transparency and jobs to stimulate the economy, but the dinosaurs learned down the road that the only stimulation benefitted the wealthy dinosaur bankers and donors. The Wall Street bankers became wealthier as they padded their fat little wallets. It was hard for the Elders to witness the Judeo-Christian dinosaurs believe Obamasaurus, when he stated that he could part the oceans and walk on water and that he had a light shining down on him.

Of course, Dinomoses didn't trust Obamasaurus and wanted to know his true identity. The media shunned anyone who criticized Obamasaurus. They were being silenced and told not to ask about his certified Birth Certificate. If they inquired, they were quickly shut down by the dino-media and accused of being "birthers" and "conspiracy theorists" as he was totally protected by the dino-news.

As time passed, Dinomoses believed that the majority of Judeo-Christian dinosaurs bought into the dangerous idea that tolerance and political correctness was a good thing, but he knew that tolerance and correctness meant even immoral and illicit and illegal acts were to be tolerated and as politically correct. Dinomoses refused to give up. He was in God's army and on a mission to share God's Ten Commandments that he believed were being eliminated. The Justices and Judges dismissed any cases requesting that the Birth Certificate be made transparent and vetted, but they dismissed every case as "no standing" and refused to uphold the Judeo-Christian Supreme Laws of the land that require eligibility. They chose to be derelict in the duty to uphold the established eligibility law.

Dinomoses recalled when his dinosaur grandpa told him the story of how God warned the Judeo-Christian dinosaurs that a reptilian dinosaur would seduce millions of Judeo-Christian dinosaurs with false promises and millions of Judeo-Christian dinosaurs would elect him in the year 2008 B.C. The wealthy reptilians who were against God and all God created would slip the foreign enemy into the highest office in the land to help them implement their depopulation agendas of all Judeo-Christians from the earth and heterosexuals as well as unborn babies and euthanize the elderly, sick, and mentally challenged.

He recalled that his dinosaur grandpa said millions would be blinded and unable to see the truth, even if they read the law, they would say, "Who cares about a silly law?" They would say, "Who cares if he isn't a natural-born Judeo-Christian dinosaur stealing the Birthright of an eligible natural born Judeo-Christian dinosaur who is innate to the soil on his Homeland and endured to his natural-born fellow citizens? God wanted that a natural-born baby born on Judeo-Christian Dinosaur soil to 2 legal Judeo-Christian dinosaurs would love their country more and their fellow citizens and defend their country and citizens more than a foreign-born dinosaur who would be town between his Homeland and his family born in his Homeland and the land he resided in legally or illegally.

In fact, Obamasaurus once stated that if the winds blew in an ugly direction that he would choose his foreign-born country and citizens over the Judeo-Christian Dinosaur Nation, but for some reason, the Judeo-Christian dinosaurs didn't appear to hear anything he said that were clues that his loyalties remained across the oceans.

The truth was concealed. Obamasaurus didn't inform the Dinosaur Nation that part of his transformation included opening up the borders to dangerous illegal foreigners and anti-Judeo-Christian immigrants and refugees. He didn't explain that he wanted to transform the dinosaur's Judeo-Christian religion into a foreign ideology that worshipped a foreign messiah. The Judeo-Christian dinosaurs didn't understand that once the dinosaurs opened the flood gates to radical foreign dinosaurs that they would be vulnerable to their stated and etched in stone goal, which was to dominate the Judeo-Christian Dinosaur Nation and wipe them off the face of the map.

They patted themselves on the back and said, "I'm a tolerant dinosaur and you are an intolerant dinosaur. This was the beginning of pitting the Judeo-Christian Dinosaurs against each other. In other words this was the beginning of their demise, if Obamasaurus and his wealthy Wall Street dino-bankers got Obamasaurus elected. They achieved their goal to redistribute the nation's wealth to themselves without the Judeo-Christians around in the future. Could that possibly happen to an entire nation by atheist men who aren't moral or ethical, but sold their souls to the reptilian snake believing they will control the world one day with fewer dinosaurs?

The Tablets stated that many Judeo-Christian dinosaurs didn't believe the truth. But, the Obamasaurus supporters promoted "tolerance" and "political correctness" and far too many Judeo-Christian dinosaurs turned their backs on their nation's laws, traditions, and roots. Obamasaurus informed the Dinosaur Nation during an interview on "Meet the Dino-Press" that he seeks to disarm their nation while trafficking guns to his foreign nation of radicals through open borders. The majority of dinosaur voters didn't pay any attention to his words and dismissed the truth. The elder dinosaurs worried it would be too late if

Obamasaurus was elected into office. If anyone questioned his agenda, they were labeled as racist not as patriots upholding the law.

Although, Obamasaurus and his regime didn't conceal that their goal was to change the Judeo-Christian majority of light and medium skin dinosaurs into a majority of foreign immigrants, refugees, and illegal dinosaurs, the majority of Judeo-Christian dinosaurs didn't appear to hear anything he said. Dinomoses wondered why the voters didn't bother to ask Obamasaurus why he sought to fulfill his foreign-born real father's dreams raising the question who was his real father? After all, Obamasaurus said he only met his dinosaur dad once in his life time. Yet, his life's goal was to fulfill the dreams of a dinosaur dad or alleged dads who were missing in action.

Noah learned that Dinomoses asked, "How can Obamasaurus be eligible to be our leader if he admitted his dinosaur father is foreign born?" But, Dinomoses stated that his question fell on deaf ears. He was called a "dino-birther" which was an attack on his intelligence used to discredit him by inferring he's from the old school.

Noah read that the dino-reporter failed to investigate Obamasaurus or even ask, "Who are you?" They didn't bother to ask, "Where were you born?" They didn't ask, "Where are your credentials?" The dino-reporters didn't ask, "How can Obamasaurus be an elected leader of the Judeo-Christian Dinosaur Nation since he stated that his dad is foreign born and that his dad's place of birth was colonized by a foreign nation. This made Obamasaurus, a Subject of that foreign nation at birth when he inherited his Birthright." Instead, the Judeo-Christian Dinosaur Nation's citizens were informed that any questions relating to the eligibility of Obamasaurus was off limits." This was the beginning of silencing free speech and ending honest elections in the Judeo-Christian Dinosaur Nation.

Noah was infatuated with the Judeo-Christian Dinosaur Legend carved into the Tablets chiseled into ancient stone. The secret Tablets revealed Obamasaurus gave a speech that included the wealthy dino-celebrities.

Obamasaurus attended a dinner with celebrities seen on the televisaurus. He laughed and stated, "I'll fly dino-birds over your houses to spy on you," but the dino-celebrities believed he was joking, but he was not joking. He was laughing at them as they laughed and applauded.

The enamored celebrities didn't realize Obamasaurus was serious. A few weeks later, Obamasaurus ordered dino-birds to fly over their homes and spy on the Judeo-Christian Dinosaur citizens. They still didn't get it. The Obamasaurus team used same-sex agendas as the catalyst that sucked them into voting for him. Noah thought of him as Santa Claus. They didn't understand that all the free giveaways would cost freedom and liberty and the loss of their Judeo-Christian Nation and possibly enact depopulation agendas.

Consequently, the conservatives and the Judeo-Christian dinosaurs were disturbed when their leader, Obamasaurus and assistant Dino-jb called a Town Hall Meeting mandating everyone attend. Obamasaurus recited his "Chicken Little" speech. They placed fear in the minds of the dinosaurs by suggesting that the sky was falling. Obamasaurus misled the dinosaurs into believing that climate change would destroy their food and water supply and threaten their very survival if they didn't elect him. He led them to believe he could swoop down as a super dino-hero and save the dinosaur citizens from themselves. Emotions ran high and they believed his fairy tale because they wanted to believe it.

Consequently, the carvings etched in the Tablets revealed that the dinosaur sheeple did elect Obamasaurus and his assistant Dinojb, but Dinomoses knew it was rigged. They misled the dinosaurs into believing that the sky was falling. Climate change was about to destroy their food and water supplies and their health. The dino-media and the "Chicken Little" story worked for them. They were able to fear monger and sell snake oil to the Judeo-Christian Nation of sheeple who ignored voter fraud and vetting laws. They never bothered to ask for his educational Degrees or his background or certified and vetted Birth Certificate or Marriage License. They didn't ask to vet his Law License or Ph.D. declaring himself to be a scholar and Professor of Law.

Obamasaurus felt empowered realizing that the dinosaur citizens were willing to buy his gig with all the media glitz. In fact, he promised to provide for all the necessities of life for the Judeo-Christian natural-born citizens. He lied. He said, "You won't have to face poverty, famine, or drought despite any climate change. You won't have to worry about being homeless. He promised them a free phoneasaurus and an autosaurus. He promised kids a dino-bike. He promised that every dinosaur would be provided with food, water, shelter, and health care. He said the government would take care of them and their dinosaur kids. Dinapeggysaurus cried tears of joy believing that she would never have to work again. Obamasuaurs and Dinojb would take care of all her needs and pay her rent and gas, but Dinomoses and the Elders knew that wasn't going to happen.

Of course, Obamasuarus promised to provide for all their needs, but the takers didn't realize that he wasn't paying for anything. The redistribution of wealth would be taken from the workers and given to the takers who wanted a free ride. Dinomoses was upset. He knew that nothing is free because someone must work and pay for the give-away programs. Obamasaurus mandated that the dinosaur workers give the bulk of their earnings to him. He intended to give their earnings away to the takers who voted for him. He stated that he was imposing higher taxes to enact the "Redistribution of Wealth" to the wealthy and the illegal foreigners that he invited to enter illegally into the nation without vetting. He said that the dinosaur citizens were too small-minded to think for themselves, but the truth was that he was enslaving the Judeo-Christian dinosaur citizens.

In reality, the slackers were taking from the worker bees under the guise of the "Redistribution of Wealth" thinking the government was paying for their necessities of life which is called "Socialism," but in fact, the fellow citizens were paying for Obamasaurus and Dinojb's necessities of life forever and everyone who was receiving the freebies. The dinosaur Judeo-Christian citizens were being hood winked and forced to pay for the living expenses for millions of illegals and radicals they migrated into their nation.

The Obamasaurus freebie program which the uneducated believed was being supplied from Obamasaurus made himself appear as a super Hero but that was not true. He was creating an illusion in order to indoctrinate the takers as his built-in voter base. These agendas led his voters into believing that they were "entitled." They truly believed they were entitled to the wealth created by the worker bees who were being enslaved. In fact, Obamasaurus and Dinojb were broke when they entered public office and soon became part of the 1% of the wealthy elite. The takers were pitted against the worker bees. The worker bees were called racists and deplorables by the Liberals and the takers who didn't work and took the freebies even though they were healthy, but told they were entitled.

After the elections, millions of dinosaurs were still mesmerized by Obamasaurus after he replaced Dinomoses as their Ruler. Millions of Judeo-Christian Dinosaurs resisted working. They believed Obamasaurus would take care of them for the rest of their lives, but they were duped. According to the Tablets, Obamasaurus was imposing mandates that would ration and deny food, water, health care, and shelter to the Judeo-Christian dinosaurs.

In fact, Obamasaurus and his committee of 9 would determine who lives and who dies. They mandated euthanasia for the sick, elderly, mentally and physically challenged. Many resisted his agendas and refused to vote for Obamasaurus and Dinojb. They didn't believe the promises that he and Dinojb would provide for all their necessities of life in exchange for their votes.

In fact, one female dinosaur council member stated on the televisaurus that Obamasaurus owed her dinosaur city, bacon, and they were coming to collect the bacon in exchange for their votes. According to the dinosaur council member, he promised a redistribution of wealth for their votes. After the Town Hall meeting, Dinochris, a male dino-reporter defended Obamasaurus. He commented that Obamasaurus sent chills up his leg. The reporter's comment caused rumors to fly and the globalist and the dinosaurs questioned if Obamasaurus was heterosexual or in the closet and if his marriage and kids were borrowed for theatrics and for optics.

One day, a female dino-reporter published an article that stated, "I couldn't help but overhear what Dinajane said on the news. She said that Obamasaurus was gay and his partner was a trans human. The Liberals were extremely upset over that statement and sadly a few weeks later, Dinjane was reported to have died which created more theories and questions and gossip. Another female dino-reporter stated, "I couldn't help but admire Dinobari and his muscular and glistening pectorals." It was obvious that the dino-media were about 98% bias in favor of their magnificent unidentified new leader, Obamasaurus.

Consequently, the dino-media made sure that every story mentioning Obamasaurus was sugar coated. Anyone who produced any negative stories ended up discredited and their stories scrubbed from the news. In fact, the leaders and the dino-media held Obamasaurus above the laws and exempted him from investigations and downplayed any allegations of investigations or punishment. The only televisaurus dino-news station who attempted to expose the truth was ROX on the Dino-News. The dino-reporters would challenge any scandals that implicated Obamasaurus except for Dinosean, who was the key host on ROX, but his messages fell on deaf ears. Noah wondered how so many of the Judeo-Christian dinosaurs could not understand how vulnerable their nation was to depopulation.

Dinomoses was disturbed by Obamasaurus catering to anti-Judeo-Christian enemy nations as well as granting millions of foreign anti-Judeo-Christian foreigners the right to migrate into their Judeo-Christian Dinosaur Nation illegally. Of course, Dinomoses realized that the dino-media would discredit him if he dared speak out against Obamasaurus.

The rumor in the Judeo-Christian Nation was dim. They reported that Obamasaurus and his regime threatened to punish any dino-reporter who dared oppose Obamasaurus. After this rumor spread, the dino-reporters feared speaking out against Obamasaurus and his senior advisor who never left his side, Dinavalerie. In fact, Dinavalerie was reported in the dino-news that anyone who opposed them would be punished. How could this happen to the Judeo-Christian Nation?

The rumors spread like wildfire. Dinosaur citizens whispered to each other as they began to fear their new leader. They feared protesting in public or marching, praying in public or even sharing their thoughts. The Tablets revealed that a few of the conservative dino-reporters warned that Obamasaurus planned on monitoring and spying on the Judeo-Christian dinosaur citizens. He even created a domestic enemy list and a domestic kill list of Judeo-Christian dinos. The NDAA Law denies due process of law and based on accusation can force innocent dinosaurs to end up in prison.

The Tablets revealed that a few of the conservative dino-reporters warned the dinosaur citizens that the Obamasaurus-regime threatened to monitor the thoughts of Judeo-Christian dinosaur citizens, but they didn't believe them. In fact, the dinosaur reporters informed the dinosaurs that they could be indefinitely detained if accused of thinking thoughts in opposition to the Obamasaurus regime as they were developing the "Thought" machines, but the majority of dino-citizens refused to believe that there was such a machine.

One bold dinosaur attorney, Dinophil, gathered important information and announced to the Judeo-Christian Dinosaur Nation that he filed an eligibility lawsuit in the dinosaur courts. In fact, one Dino-reporter stated, "Any dinosaur, who believes that Obamasaurus isn't telling the truth about his identity, is making false and bogus statements."

The magnificent dinosaur, who introduced himself as Obamasaurus never disclosed his secret agendas during his campaign. He waited until he accessed the highest office in their land and presented himself as a prominent active lawyer and expert on the Judeo-Christian Supreme Laws. He stated he was a Professor of Law at a famous University of Law. He failed to mention that he and his wife's law licenses had been revoked after a criminal investigation by the Dino's State Bar Disciplinary Board. A credentialed and well-respected prosecutor, Dinophil, alleged that Obamasaurus and his wife were prohibited from practicing law throughout the Judeo-Christian Dinosaur Nation. He alleged that there wasn't any proof that the new leader was a Professor of Law, but a substitute on rare occasion.

Furthermore, attorney Dinophil, learned that the foreign-born dinosaur dad named Obamasaurus, sr. was already married with children living in Kenyaville prior to allegedly marrying his light skin dinosaur mom, born in the Judeo-Christian nation, which would have been prohibited by law at the time. These actions would mean that the light skin dinosaur teenage mom and the dark skin adult male alleged to be the foreign-born dad of Obamasaurus would equate to having committed the crimes of bigamy and adultery and a violation of the segregation laws that had been implemented at the time in the Judeo-Christian nation.

Attorney Dinophil alleged that the Judeo-Christian dinosaurs would remember a dark skin dinosaur dating a light skin teenage dinosaur back in the day when a light skin dinosaur female wasn't allowed to even speak to a dark skin dinosaur. Attorney Dinophil stated that such behavior wouldn't have gone unnoticed by the students, school or dinosaur citizens and such behavior would probably cause riots and arrests and possibly injury. Emotions would have run high on both sides.

Dinomoses read that the dinosaur dad of Obamasaurus practiced a foreign religion that prohibited a light skin female dinosaur born in a Judeo-Christian nation from marrying a dark skin dinosaur of their nation unless the light skin Judeo-Christian dinosaur and her dinosaur son converted to his dino-stepdad's foreign religion. Non-compliance under the dinosaur stepdad's foreign religion would have resulted in punishment for the light skin dinosaur mom, so Dinomoses wondered if Dinobari may resent his mom for removing him from a Judeo-Christian Nation and from his former school after he was allegedly brought to live in the Judeo-Christian Nation once they left Kenyaville after his birth.

Nevertheless, during the campaign, Obamasaurus and his supporters presented Obamasaurus and his wife as a heterosexual Traditional Married couple with 2 dino-kids. He stated to the Dinosaur Nation that he believed in Traditional Marriage and that he supported pro-life and he lied.

In fact, after the elections, the elders of the Judeo-Christian Dinosaur Nation learned that Obamasaurus signed a worldwide mandated abortion law which required the dinosaur citizens of the Judeo-Christian Dinosaur nation to comply with mandated abortions, or else be punished. Dinomoses feared that mandated abortions of future Judeo-Christian dinosaurs could lead to depopulation. Obamasaurus also flip flopped and supported same-sex dinosaur marriages after elections and enforced same sex indoctrination into schools and into the Judeo-Christian Dinosaur Nation's military by the year 2009 B.C., which are depopulation programs of the Judeo-Christian natural-born babies.

Some of the Tablets were difficult to decipher, but Noah managed to uncover the fact that Dinomoses grew weary and restless knowing the truth about Obamasaurus. Dinomoses would stay up late. He'd sit at his stone-age desk carving notes into stone under a flickering light from pieces of wood that he rubbed together and threw into the fireplace. His mind was on over load. Many times, Dinomoses fell asleep with his head on the desk.

Dinomoses was quite disturbed as rumors spread that Obamasaurus preferred same sex relationships outside of his marriage which hit the globalist dino-tabloids. In fact, Dinolarry, wrote a book about his former friend, Obamasaurus. In the book, Dinolarry alleged that he and Obamasaurus were involved in a same sex relationship and used illegal herbs, but the dino-media remained silent and ignored the shocking book so it would be forgotten.

Noah was fascinated when he read that the dinosaur mom of Obamasaurus left him alone quite frequently with a cross-dressing dinosaur nanny after his mom re-married. She married another foreign-born man who was also attending the same university as Obama's alleged first dad, Obamasaurus, sr., so that appeared to be a strange coincidence. The two men belonged to the same religion and lived in the Middle East and were in the Judeo-Christian Nation at the same time on student loans. Obamasaurus light skin dino-mom married his stepdad, Dinololo.

Some say that the birth of Dinobari also known as Obamasaurus was pre planned to create a white-black dinosaur birth created by foreign enemy leaders from faraway lands who sought to conquer the Judeo-Christian Nation in the future. The rumor was that they would groom him and mentor him on anti-Judeo-Christian foreign ideologies, same-sex, cross-dressing, Judeo-Christian Laws and anti-Judeo-Christian foreign religions and fund his education and upkeep.

The Tablet symbols indicated that Obamasaurus' mom moved from the Judeo-Christian Nation of her birth to a foreign nation across the oceans who were anti-Judeo-Christian and married the stepdad to Obamasaurus named Dinololo. It was their nation's law that required Obamasaurus to become a legal citizen of that foreign nation and that the child relinquish any other citizenship to a foreign land in order to attend school in their nation. Judeo-Christian teachings were prohibited. So, the stepdad, Dinololo legally adopted Obamasaurus. He changed his stepson's name legally to Dinobari-lolo. This would require Dinobari to repatriate himself upon his return to Kenyaville or to the Judeo-Christian Nation in the future.

Noah decoded information that stated there wasn't any proof that the alleged parents of Obamasaurus were his biological dinosaur parents. He never produced any evidence of his birth or proof of his biological parents or proof of his birth place or birth date. The story read that the dinosaur mom was reported to be an atheist and a communist dinosaur.

There wasn't proof that the light skin dinosaur mom of Obamasaurus converted to the alleged foreign-born dad's religion or that his foreign-born dinosaur dad was accused of bigamy, adultery, or violating segregation laws. There wasn't any proof that at any point, Dinobari repatriated himself as Obamasaurus in the Judeo-Christian Nation upon re-entry as a foreign-national.

Dinomoses listened to a speech by Obamasaurus when he stated that his alleged foreign-born dad believed that the Judeo-Christian Dinosaur Nation was oppressive. In fact, the Tablets stated that the majority of dinosaurs who were family members, friends, mentors, and associates close to Obamasaurus during his entire life time were reported in the dino-news to be radicals, socialists, communists, and criminals. Some of his associates ended up in Femasaurus Camps after they were prosecuted for wrong doing such as Dinotony and Dinorob who were close associates of Obamasaurus and he didn't bother to pardon them after he was elected.

Noah read that Dinomoses completed his research on the background of Obamasaurus. He called for a clandestine meeting of the elders to be held at his home. After the elections of 2008 B.C. Dinomoses felt oppressed and silenced by the new regime. In fact, he recalled an article that stated Obamasaurus visited a major dino-news agency and afterwards, the dino-news agency refused to release an important news story prior to elections.

There were other dino-news articles that stated Obamasaurus attended Rev. Dinoright's Judeo-Christian church. He became a controversial figure when he hit the news stating "god d....the Judeo Christian Nation, not God Bless the Judeo-Christian Nation." And then the news reported that 3 young friends of Dinobari who sang in the dino-choir attended the same church and the dino-news reported they were found dead prior to the elections. Ironically, his light skinned dinosaur grandmother died one day after he visited her in the hospital which was a day before his inauguration. Almost everyone associated or related to Obamasaurus who knew his history from birth to the day of election inside the Judeo-Christian Nation seemed to have died or were jailed or silent. His light skin Judeo-Christian dinosaur mother died. His alleged dark-skinned relations included his dino-dad and dino-stepdad and dino-stepsister. It must have been very sad and lonely for Obamasaurus after his light skin dino-grandparents died and his light skin dino-mom. He also lost his dark skin dino-dad and dark dark skin dino-stepdad as well as his dino-stepsister. Dinobari's 2 dino-friends, Dinotony and Dinorob were jailed. All but one of these deaths and arrests occurred prior to the inauguration.

Dinomoses addressed the elders and said, "The Judeo-Christian youth of voting age view Obamasaurus as a Rock Star!" Noah was intrigued with the carvings that he was decoding carved into the stone. He thought it's obvious that Obamasuaurus had a secret desire to be a Rock Star. He could dance and he could sing. Obamasaurus enjoyed the limelight on the televisaurus more than being a leader. He liked jammin' in the spotlight with Dinojimmie or Dinodavid or Dinoleno which aired on the late night televisaurus. Mrs. Obamasaurus enjoyed rocking out on Dinaellen's show or Dinabarbara's show during the day. The young dinosaurs loved it.

Consequently, there were many Judeo-Christian dinosaurs, such as Peggysaurus, who believed that Obamasaurus was her savior. For example, a dino-reporter asked Peggysaurus, "Why did you vote for Obamasaurus?" Peggysaurus replied, "Mr. Obamasaurus is going to provide for all my necessities of life. He's going to pay for my rock style home and provide me with a free dinophone, free food and water, and national health care, even, free herbal contraceptives and abortions. I don't ever have to work again." Of course, there was Dinojoplumer, who owned a small business and spoke out against the redistribution of wealth which he felt would hurt many of the Judeo-Christian good hearted dinosaurs. The Judeo-Christian Nation was a Republic and operated by the Rule of Law and established Free Enterprise and Capitalism. Obamasaurus was attempting not just to change and transform the Judeo-Christian Dinosaur Nation into Socialism and Communism, but Globalism with fewer dinosaurs to control.

Nonetheless, even with all the unanswered questions about Dinobari also known as Obamasaurus, the unanswered questions about his background and place of birth and his real names and credentials were never made transparent and they remained a mystery to the Elders so his eligibility was never proven.

The Judeo-Christian Dinosaur citizens who didn't vote for him didn't trust him.

One day, Sheriff Dinojoe and Obamasaurus were on the dino-news and Sheriff Dinojoe asked Obamasaurus why he and Dinojb aren't securing the borders as required by law and Obamasaurus laughed. He said, "What do you want me to do? I could dig a molt and fill it with alligators."

The dinosaurs discussed the weather when it was too hot or too cold, but they weren't familiar with the new buzz words, "Global Warming," being made so common or "climate change" which became major buzz words under the Obamasaurus regime. Most of the Judeo-Christian dinosaurs never questioned their leaders because life in the past was basic and simple and they were content with the lifestyle in the nation that they created for themselves and future generations of Judeo-Christian dinosaurs. However, the Elders were very concerned about the young dinosaurs who fell for the Obamasaurus and Dinojb's fairy tale stories.

Dinomoses met with other Elders and Sheriff Dinojoe and Officer Dinomac and Dinojb and Dinodon over coffee. Dinomoses said, "Obamasaurus suddenly appeared in the Judeo-Christian Dinosaur Nation like a bolt of lightning as if he flew in on a magical carpet from an exotic foreign land unknown to us."

Dinojob remarked, "I recall hearing rumors of an exotic land across the oceans where magical carpets were used by their magicians and prophets who created spells made from herbs and that they had some sort of power to make carpets fly. They can control snakes by musical sounds. They can even see into the future and far away lands through a crystal ball. I don't believe it, but I did hear stories."

Dinomoses said, "Well, let's not go that far. We've already heard enough fairy tales from Obamasaurus and his side kick, Dinojb. But, we do have to admit that he did mesmerize the female dinosaurs when he arrived and targeted the youth with basketball, bike rides, golf, and convinced them that change and transformation was the New Age of the future. He encouraged the dino-youth to dismiss the elders as old school."

Sheriff Diinojoe said, "Well, it's not unusual to see Obamasaurus out on the green open grass playing a game of dino-golf. He actually has a set of golf clubs that I noticed were made out of red wood and they noted that his name, "Dinobari" was engraved on each golf stick. He must have practiced a lot because the young dinosaurs noticed that he had a great swing and was pretty good on the golf course when he joined Dinogeorge and Dinogaites and Dinojb.

Obamasaurus Frequents the Golf Course

CHAPTER 9

Changing a Nation's Behaviors

Over time, the natural-born dinosaur citizens of the Dinosaur Nation began to wake up and realize that they made a disastrous mistake, but it was too late. Obamasaurus won the election with the help of a group he formed as their community organizer known as Dinoacorn. And, Obamasaurus was their mentor prior to the elections. Ironically, many of the members of Dinoacorn ended up charged by Officer Dinomack with voter fraud after the elections.

They helped Obamasaurus commit a fraudulent election, but there wasn't much they could do about it because they claimed there weren't any laws that addressed fraudulent elections and foreign spies accessing the highest office in the land after elected.

The Elders acknowledged that Obamasaurus was an eloquent speaker. He didn't miss a beat and he always came up with the right answers to the questions when asked by the dinosaur citizens or the dino-press. He knew when to turn a bad question into a joke and make the dinosaur citizens and the dino-press laugh.

In fact, he spoke out of both sides of his mouth which confused the dinosaur citizens and the dino-press. He even stated that he used more of his reptilian side of his brain to make important decisions and convinced the dinosaur citizens and the press with his charm that it was a good thing to make important decisions with the reptilian side of his brain.

The dino-youth applauded and the adult dinosaurs who voted for him. Someone in the audience yelled, "You're Satan" and disrupted his speech, but he just looked at the dino-male and it was very strange as he was calm and didn't deny it, he just let the security remove him from the press conference.

Obamasaurus, The President

Obviously, the Judeo-Christian dinosaur citizens didn't realize that Obamasaurus would mandate laws against the will of the majority of citizens after elections. They didn't realize that he would impose laws which could eliminate their Freedoms and Liberties and Rights. The dinosaur citizens weren't aware of his disdain for free enterprise, entrepreneurship, and his desire to compete in a world of dino-capitalism along with his wealthy donors and bankers.

The dinosaur citizens weren't aware that the worker bees would be mandated to pay about 80% of their earnings in food and water supplies to Obamasaurus and his regime for redistribution of wealth, to him and his wealthy donors and bankers. They were about to outsource their jobs and hard work and their intellectual property and inventions that included bikes, weapons, water supply equipment, and food and water to foreign anti-Judeo-Christian Nations without benefit to the Judeo-Christian dinosaurs.

Noah yawned and stretched as he had to break from decoding the Tablets.

The hours past quickly. He drank some water and ate a sandwich and decided to hike back to camp before it got dark. He was overwhelmed with what he had already learned about the dinosaur legend. After resting his tired eyes, he packed up and began his hike down the hill which he didn't mind since it was much easier hiking down the mountainside than up the long dusty trail that led to the secret cave. Afterwards, he hiked back to camp where he'd rest and get his notes together. He was elated with what he discovered.

He walked over to the campfire and lit the wood and waited for the fire to start while he waited for his dinner to heat up. He settled into a a small folding chair and continued reading a book that he brought with him while the coffee perked and the chile was heating up. Several minutes later, he ate a plate of chile and then poured a cup of hot coffee with sugar and cream. He could hear the birds and other animal noises in the jungles. He never let his guard down knowing he could face an unwelcome visitor. He enjoyed the nights and the jungle noises before falling asleep.

The next morning, he performed the same routine. And, he headed towards the trail that led to the cave because his time was limited before he would have to return to the states, so what was the secret message that Dr. Lee stated he needed to take back to the American people. His passion drove him to find that message before the possibility of depopulation or extinction came upon humanity. He arrived and unpacked and sat down next to the Tablets.

The Tablets read that since time began, the Judeo-Christian dinosaurs were smart because they created wealth by growing and storing vegetables and fruits and herbs and water for winter and possibly a drought one day as the weather is unpredictable. Noah thought for a moment. Food. Water. Sunshine. Rain. Fresh Clean Air. These are the essentials all species need to preserve their species including the Bees, plants and Trees.

Judeo-Christian dinosaurs gained wealth by growing and storing veggies and fruits, water, and herbs, but now they were threatened by Obamasaurus and his wealthy donors and bankers who sought to own all the food, water, health care herbs needed for their survival in the Judeo Christian Nation of dinosaurs.

Unfortunately, the Judeo-Christian dinosaurs didn't listen to their Elders and they were unaware that their hard work and savings would be pilfered by Obamasaurus. It appeared that these wealthy donors and his regime were seeking to create a famine and thirst as they were working to control the water and the land and food under the guise of Redistribution of Wealth.

The new programs implemented by the unidentified magnificent dinosaur mandated that the wealth for dinosaurs was determined by their food and water supplies. The redistribution was to be sent to anti-Judeo-Christian foreign nations through the U.N., aka United Nomads. Dinomoses stated, "Our Judeo-Christian Dinosaur Nation can't survive if the workers must give up everything they earn to their leaders so they can redistribute our supplies to foreign anti-Judeo-Christian dinosaurs. Dinomoses said, "The well will run dry and all the Judeo-Christian dinosaurs could die."

The dinosaur Tablets read that after the elections, Obamasaurus swore an oath to uphold the original Judeo-Christian laws established by the Dinosaur Nation. In fact, he swore the oath twice, once in public, and once in private without the Judeo-Christian Tablet present when Justice dino-rob administered the oath that Obamasaurus laughed about and flubbed up in public.

Ironically, after Obamasaurus took office, he kept his promise for the first six months and he supplied the dinosaurs with natural organic food and clean water. But he secretly wrote an amendment to the law and granted illegal authority to conceal his identity from the Judeo-Christian Dinosaur Nation without objection by the dino-congress. They were the only body allowed by law to make laws, approve laws and abide by the laws they approve, not Obamasaurus running the nation by Mandates. But, no one objected in the dino-congress or the dino-senate and allowed him to enact a dictatorial free reign of terror coming to the Judeo-Christian Dinosaur Nation. The storm was coming soon.

Obamasaurus enacted his own healthcare mandates and promised he would provide healthy organic medicinal herbs to the dino-citizens. He said, "My dinosaur czars will provide for all the dino-citizens who pay up-front for health care services, which can be rationed and denied without recourse depending upon the decision by the healthcare czars. The Elders knew that dinogaites and dinogeorge were hoping to euthanize the elderly and very sick and mentally and physically challenged as part of their depopulation program of the Judeo-Christians and those they found to be obsolete or undesirables in their eyes.

Furthermore, the elders realized that Obamasaurus failed to disclose that the dinosaurs, who didn't comply and pay-up-front, would be punished. He didn't disclose that his health care plan provided for death panels and that his "Committee of 9" would choose, who will live or die, by rationing or denying health care services or treatments to the Judeo-Christian dinosaur citizens. Since, he kept his promise to provide them with their daily needs after elected into office, the youth of the Dinosaur Nation didn't understand what they were giving up.

The Judeo-Christian dinosaurs would be required to relinquish their individualism, freedom, liberty, property, kids, weapons, religion, privacy, right-to-life, right to the pursuit of happiness, unalienable rights, maintaining a sovereign nation as well as due process of law, in exchange for the entitlement programs promised by the Obamasaurus regime. They were also required to comply with a foreign political ideology under the guise of religion.

Dinomoses said, "It's my opinion that the Obamasaurus health care programs will lead to collectivism, entitlement programs, and unconstitutional laws leaving the Judeo-Christian Dinosaur Nation vulnerable to abuses and injustices. He could leave us rationing everything.

Unfortunately, the free nation didn't get it soon enough! The Obamasaurus unvetted czars would evaluate dinosaurs as commodities for-profit. The unidentified liberal czars would evaluate Judeo-Christian dinosaurs as to their worth and lack of worth. The Elders worried that Obamasaurus intended to turn the Judeo-Christian citizens into slaves or worker bees and they would be treated as chattel while foreign dark dinosaurs would migrate into their nation by the millions and dominate their land. The citizens of the Judeo-Christian Dinosaur Nation such as the elderly, sick, old guard, disabled, and unborn babies would be depopulated by attrition. Obamasaurus exempted the Left and targeted the Judeo-Christians.

The Judeo-Christian dinosaur's history book would be changed and replaced. The foreign anti-Judeo-Christian leaders seeking to dominate would state that the Judeo-Christian Dinosaur Nation was conquered and no longer exists.

Dinomoses was sitting at home in his rock cave watching ROX news. He was trying to remain logical and figure out how to begin an exodus from the Judeo-Christian Nation and save as many Judeo-Christian Dinosaurs as possible, but he had to figure out how to do it without being noticed. His plan was to take male and female dinosaurs who were willing to leave in an attempt to save their dinosaur species. First he needed a plan and a strategy. He needed to contact dinosaurs that were trustworthy and would help find a place for the refugee dinosaurs to flee without being arrested for violating their new curfew laws laid out by Obamasaurus and his dino-regime. He decided to call a meeting of the Elders only and determine who is trustworthy and who shouldn't be informed of this movement for life and freedom. This was a dangerous and bold agenda, but Dinomoses and the Elders were fearless warriors and crusaders. They believed that their Judeo-Christian God would guide them to a safe and secret place that would be undetectable by the foreign and domestic enemies. He felt better after making a decision and grabbed his hot cup of chamomile tea and a book and headed for bed.

CHAPTER 10

President Obamasaurus Signs Mandates

Rationing Food and Drinks

After the dust settled, the Tablets disclosed that Mrs. Obamasaurus showed up on the scene. She announced that every dinosaur citizen would be required to change their behaviors, especially their eating and drinking behaviors. She introduced her new program to the Judeo-Christian dinosaurs. She said. "My dinosaur czars will decide what you can or cannot eat and drink." For example, she informed the youth that they must do as dinosaur Mayor, Dinomike, mandated. Dinosaurs will no longer be allowed to buy 32ounce beverages.

The dinosaur citizens were shocked. After all, they did enjoy dinosaur size drinks, especially the 32 oz. bottles of berry juices, not just water. They also enjoyed fish and fowl upon occasion, not just vegetables. It didn't take long before Mr. and Mrs. Obamasaurus prohibited certain snacks and rationed food, water, and health care. It appeared to Dinomoses that they were attempting to ration food so dinosaurs would get use to eating less food and drinking less liquid as well.

The Obamasaurus regime issued mandates and requirements for all Judeo-Christian dinosaurs to follow. The new leader declared that if the Judeo-Christian dinosaurs failed to comply with his mandates, they would be punished for non-compliance and locked away in Femasaurus camps where they would attend classes on how to behave as required by the new mandates. Also, the elderly, sick, disabled, mentally challenged and old military guard could be denied or rationed health care services and could be targeted for early end-of-life counseling or psychiatric treatment which included veterans, parents and grandparents.

The dinosaur Mayor, Dinorahm, as well as Obamasaurus believed that early end-of-life was a good policy. He believed that if dinosaur kids ended up as orphans that they should be molded and indoctrinated into the government's ideologies and required to join the Dinosaur National Civilian Security Force (DNCSF).

The behavioral changes that were to be implemented through schools by the federal dinosaur government offered substantial incentives to the state's leaders and educators. Of course, most of the dinosaur leaders accepted the incentives even if it involved treason and depopulation. Dinosaur educators couldn't resist the bribes and trampled on parental rights to decide the best interest of their own minor dinosaur kids. These were the goals issued by Obamasaurus in 2008 B.C. and his educational program.

In fact, the Obamasaurus administration proposed mandated oral vaccines injected into every dinosaur child even though they were still in development.

There was unknown consequences to individual dinosaur kids which could cause injury or death or benefit them as the consequences were unknown.

Secret Hit Lists

The citizens of the Dinosaur Nation were shocked when they learned that the unidentified Obamasaurus and his czars granted themselves absolute authority to determine which Judeo-Christian dinosaurs would be placed on a hit list for assassinations based on accusation only. The hit list didn't exclude Judeo-Christian females, elderly, or dinosaur kids. Any Judeo-Christian dinosaur accused of opposing the new leader's agendas would be denied the right to know the charges and denied a trial or the right to speak to a prominent dinosaur lawyer. The dinosaur citizens didn't have to be charged with a crime, only accused of being a domestic enemy.

The dinosaur lawyers remained silent and the dinosaur congress approved the unconstitutional tyrannical laws, as well as the Patriot Act, NDAA and radiation. On the other hand, many of the dinosaur-leaders were dinosaur lawyers who were self-regulating and self-protecting their own. They exempted themselves from the "assassination hit lists," as well, and held themselves above the immoral and unconstitutional laws they were dishing out for the Judeo-Christian dinosaurs.

The Judeo-Christian dinosaurs began to realize that Obamasaurus and his assistant Dinojb tricked them with their "Chicken Little" story and fake promises of providing for their citizens. The lies left the Elders disturbed that the Judeo-Christian leaders or faux Judeo-Christian leaders weren't charged with a potential premeditated genocide of the Judeo-Christian citizens. Fear could cause the Judeo-Christian Dinosaur Nation to be conquered by depopulation and by an exodus of those who leave before it may be too late.

As Noah read the Tablets, he felt sorry for the Judeo-Christian dinosaur citizens. He read that the Judeo-Christian Dinosaur Nation appeared to fear the unidentified dinosaur leader. It appeared that Obamasaurus granted absolute power to himself without any Judeo-Christian dinosaur member of congress stopping him even though it was an abuse of power. And, the Judeo-Christian dinosaur leaders didn't care that he granted himself authority to withhold his identity from the dino-government and the dinosaur citizens.

The Judeo-Christian wealthy donors and bankers violated the law that established and guaranteed enforcement of Article II, Sec. 1,

Clause 5, which all Judeo-Christian dinosaurs swore to uphold. Most of the Judeo-Christian dinosaurs didn't fight back or peacefully resist. They feared being placed on a "hit" list or being indefinitely detained in a Femasaurus Camp without due process of law. Fear was the biggest enemy that haunted the Judeo-Christian Dinosaur Nation's citizens. They forgot to trust God.

It wasn't long afterwards that the Elders met secretly to discuss how they could help save their Judeo-Christian Nation and citizens, but the dino-media wouldn't support them or the dino-reporters. They turned their backs on their Homeland and families and friends and fellow citizens who loved God and their Homeland. Sadly, the media sold them out which was a huge problem for the Elders who knew they must make quick decisions for those they might save.

Snitch Snack Program

Noah read that the Judeo-Christian dinosaurs had created excellent schools and that the history of their nation was part of their required curriculum. The schools provided activities and exercises as well as tasty lunches for the dinosaur children. The Tablet read as follows: One day, the teachers informed the dinosaur kids that they would be visited by the First Lady Dinosaur. The students and teachers were required to attend the event. The dinosaur kids were excited. They had been informed that the topic would be about nutrition. After everyone settled into the auditorium, Mrs. Obamasaurus approached the center of the auditorium and received a warm welcome.

The audience was silent as she stated, "Moving 'forward,' the Dinosaur schools will be expected to change their behaviors. This won't be easy, but it's part of the transformation and change that will be implemented across the Judeo-Christian Dinosaur Nation." The audience was shocked. She said, "I will head up the program and we will decide what you can or can't eat or drink. We don't want any dinosaurs wobbling through the halls of our schools. This won't be easy, but it is necessary to move forward."

The students and staff were silent. She continued, "We expect every dinosaur student to report to us if your friends, teachers, or parents are snacking on junk foods. We expect the students to report the offenders to the Snitch Snack Czar. My staff and I have determined that there are too many fat dinosaurs wobbling around this nation." She stopped and looked around at the students and said, "So, as of today, you are on notice that the head of Dino-security will be visiting the public schools randomly and making sure you are reporting everyone who cheats, so don't be a knucklehead and try to cheat."

A few days later, the Dino-reporters published a photo that was carved in stone with the story that depicted an image of Mr. and Mrs. Obamasaurus eating dino-fried chicken, dino-fried shrimp, double dinoburgers, fried dinotaters, and dinopie with a scoop of dinocream on top and a 32 oz. dino-soda pop at a nearby restaurant located in Harlem near a church with a popular dinosaur pastor, Dinojamcs-damming. The dark skin dino-pastor warned the Judeo-Christian Dinosaur Nation and the dark skin dinosaur foreign nations that in the end, everyone will suffer if they vote for Obamasaurus. Noah wasn't too surprised to decode that the dino-czars were reported in the news to be wasting resources and spying on their own Judeo-Christian citizens.

Obamasaurus Food Mandate didn't apply to him or his family or donors.

Noah was surprised when he decoded that the Judeo-Christian Dinosaur Nation's spending was excessive and spent on partying, heavy drinking, and eating plenty of unhealthy snacks, as well as, paying for dino-escorts at expensive five-star dino-resorts. They also held dino-kids pizza parties at the Obamasaurus mansion for his kid's Birthdays. It appeared that the Obamasaurus family's Snitch Snack Program only applied to the Judeo-Christian natural born dinosaurs living under the thumb of the Obamasusaurus mandates that denied their kids pizza parties. Dino-kids were also punished, not just their parents.

After the appearance by Mrs. Obamasaurus at the public schools, the principals were instructed to implement the Snitch Snack program immediately. The mandate read that a first-timc offense for violating the Snitch Snack Program resulted in a warning for a first-time offender. A second offense would result in paying a stiff penalty, and a third offense would result in being indefinitely detained at a Femasaurus camp where the accused would learn to comply with the Obamasaurus behavioral eating programs!

Thereafter, the dinosaur students and dinosaur educators stated to the students, "You can only store a minimal amount of approved government food and water in school lunches or else face punishment. And, dinosaurs cannot collect and store rain water." One teacher said, "But, the government doesn't own the rain!" The thin dinosaur's school Principal said, "The schools and parents can't grow organic vegetables or fruits on school property or private property or else they will face punishment." The Principal informed the dinosaur -students that if they violate the new rules that Mrs. Obamasaurus could send the dino-cops, a private police force, run by wealthy Dinogaites.

The dino-cops would enforce the new laws which required dino-farmcrs to buy modified seeds which didn't contain any nutritional value. Dinokisingher was pleased. He said, "This is a wonderful opportunity to create the New World Order of Dinosaurs.

One month later, Ms. Dinasebilasaurus, appeared on campus as the new health care czar. She was put in charge of the dinosaur students, moving forward. She informed the staff and students that they planned on implementing health care clinics and abortion hubs in every school. She stated that the Obamasaurus czars would be in charge of the dino-kids physical examinations, abortions, contraceptive and mandated vaccine programs. She reiterated that there wouldn't be any parental right to opt out. She said that the Obamasaurus regime would take control of the dinosaur kids health care records under the authority of the dinosaur leader's close advisor, Dinavalerie, who was born in an anti-Judeo-Christian foreign nation. She supported the agenda and approved of it.

Dinavalerie's intent was to deny all parental rights and place dinosaur kids under the authority of a foreign agency by utilizing the public schools. The foreign agency was known as the UNDA which stands for the United Nomads of the Dinosaur Assn. The students were to be molded, and told what they can or can't be, and what they can or can't do, which was the goal of the UNDA. UNDA was behind the redistribution of the wealth of the Judeo-Christian Nations and they intended to dominate their nation through depopulation programs by rationing and denying healthy foods and clean water. Of course, the dinosaur parents were shocked to hear all the changes that were being mandated without parental rights or the right for parents to opt out of programs. The Obamasaurus regime had taken control of their children as well as their health care decisions, food and drink.

The dinosaur Tablets revealed to Noah that sovereignty wasn't just a word.

The Judeo-Christian Dinosaurs and their lifestyle was being turned upside down because they didn't guard their borders. They didn't uphold their immigration laws and vetting laws. The patriotic dinosaurs realized it would be difficult for many to believe the truth and that they didn't have any idea that foreign spies had entered through the back door while they were asleep. Many of their species were good souls and never imagined that their super powerful nation could be taken down by one foreign-born dinosaur who was welcomed into the nation by the good and law-abiding citizens. The Judeo-Christian dinosaurs had forgotten that it's their God-given inalienable natural right to live free of tyranny, but they let their guard down and didn't hold their leaders accountable. The Judeo-Christian Dinosaur Nation was now at a crossroads and it was a matter of life and death. They decided to meditate and pray about their next steps to saving their species from being wiped off the face of the map. The question blowing in the wind was whether or not they could survive and save their nation.

CHAPTER 11

Food & Water regulated

Same Sex Education

After Mr. and Mrs. Obamasaurus implemented these programs, the teachers and principals, were stunned when they received instructions from their leaders informing them, that it was imperative that they begin the implementation of the new public school programs immediately. The staff felt uncomfortable when they learned that the number one goal was to commence classes on same sex lifestyles, transgender lifestyles, and cross-dressing lifestyles as well as same sex marriages and diminish the teachings of traditional marriage. This program was to be taught under the guise of health care, but many dinosaur parents believed it was an indoctrination program, not an educational program.

The school's dinosaur teachers wondered why the administrators and the dinosaur's judges weren't protecting the welfare and safety of the dinosaur kids from being exposed to sex education classes at an early age.

The natural born Judeo-Christian dinosaur parents opposed these agendas, but to no avail. This was immoral in the eyes of the Judeo-Christian dinosaur citizens and placed innocent dinosaur kids in harm's way.

Dinomoses was quite concerned about indoctrinating little kids into same sex education and robbing them of their innocence at a tender age. Dinomoses believed in freedom of choice, not denying parents freedom of choice to choose sex education and sexual preference. So, Dimonoses called the Elders. He requested that they attend a secret meeting at his home.

The Elders showed up at his home and settled in with cookies and coffee eager to discuss these immoral and disturbing agendas. After everyone arrived, Dinomoses stated, "I read that Obamasaurus and his wife are working overtime to change the behaviors of our nation's children as well as our food, drinks, and sexual behaviors even at a tender age when dinosaur kids are barely out of diapers. It's the duty of the dinosaur courts to protect the best interest of the dinosaur kids, so why aren't they performing their duty? If all kids are indoctrinated in same-sex, there will be no more natural-born Judeo-Christian babies born in the future to preserve our nation."

One way to change a nation is by controlling the dinosaur kids," stated Dinojob. "That's correct," commented Dinomoses. The room was silent for a few minutes. Dinomoses rasied his voice, "Are you aware that the unidentified czars he appointed are mandating same-sex curriculums into public schools against the will of heterosexual parents? But, Obamasaurus not only intends to implement same sex into public schools, he's pushing to implement these same classes into private Judeo-Christian Schools. They distanced boys and girls which caused dino-kids to fear speaking to each other. The school board believed this would prevent pregnancies.

Now, I'm not denying anyone their personal sexual preference, but I am concerned that they are promoting these agendas so after they depopulate the Judeo-Christian Nation, no more natural-born Judeo-Christian dinosaurs will be born making us extinct from the earth and never to be remembered in the future." Dinomoses mentioned that the Obamasaurus czars were promoting pedophilia as legal. The Elders were stunned. They asked, "But, what can we do?"

As Noah interpreted the dinosaur Tablets, he felt sick after reading these agendas, especially agendas that robbed the dinosaur kids of their innocence. Dinomoses feared that the Judeo-Christians were being forced into depopulation programs, but he didn't know what to do. He asked, "So, what can the elder dinosaurs do to stop the agendas implemented by Obamasaurus that could depopulate our nation within the next 10-15 years. Our nation could be taken over by the Obamasaurus nation. He was probably foreign-born as his grandma stated."

The Tablets revealed that any information relating to the background of Obamasaurus was very limited. One dinosaur reporter named, Dinoglenn, referred to the Obamasaurus stories as fairy tales. And then his show was removed from ROX. It was very difficult to share information with the Judeo-Christian dinosaur citizens who thought that the change and transformation was a good thing. The conservative dino-reporters stated that Obamasaurus once stated if things got really ugly that he'd have to favor his dark skin dino-dad's race and foreign nation.

Sheriff Dinojoe asked, "Shouldn't we ask, if Obamasaurus came to our nation on a mission which would be to depopulate us with domestic wealthy enemies who donate to him and to use the foreigners he migrates into the nation to overpopulate and eventually dominate until our nation is no longer recognizable and we end up as the minority if we're still alive on our Homeland?"

Obamasaurus bought up tons of weapons and Femasaurus trains so why would he do that? He also stated that he seeks to fulfill his foreign-born dino-dad's dream as he never got over being a Subject of a foreign Judeo-Christian Nation under their rule which is no one's fault in today's world. He once said that he and his dad believe that Judeo-Christian Nations are oppressive and evil. Yet, he never talks about his past or his background. He only talks about change and transformation.

Dinomoses stood up and looked around the room. He said, "Remember it was Dinanancy who stated, "We must pass the unread healthcare bill, so we can know, what's in it." She also denied that the bill included mandated taxpayer funded worldwide vaccines and abortions. How is it that they can enforce hundreds of laws, taxes, penalties, mandates, requirements, punishments, fines without reading the 2700 pages and studying each mandate to be sure it is in the best interest of the dino-citizens? Isn't that why they were elected into office?

Dinomoses commented, "We know that Obamasaurus is obsessed with mandated abortions, infanticide, and partial birth abortions which were the only bills he voted on. Maybe, he doesn't like babies. He said, in public that if his daughter made a mistake (and got pregnant) that he would want her to get an abortion. So, he was also saying that it's okay with him if his grandchild is aborted That's quite telling. Dinojob said, "Like Dinomoses said, if we don't have natural-born babies to grow up and preserve this sovereign nation, it will no longer exist."

After looking at his watch, Noah rested from decoding the dinosaur Tablets. He felt overwhelmed as usual with his discovery and the secret dinosaur legend, so he decided to pack up and head back to camp and write more notes and get some rest before heading back to the cave in the morning.

The hours in the cave flew by. He made it back to camp and wrote some short letters to his friends in the states and would drop them off in the village early and pick up some more food and other supplies while he was there before heading back to camp. He looked forward to 8 hours of sleep and feeling energized in the morning.

Noah washed up the next morning and grabbed his backpack and peddled to the village where he ate a hot breakfast, Orange Juice and coffee, and picked up what he needed. He dropped off his letters for the mail carrier and peddled back to camp where he dropped off the supplies and he grabbed his walking stick and headed back to the cave hoping he was getting close to the message he needed to discover. After Noah arrived back inside the cave, he pulled out a camping chair and found where he left off on the Tablet. He learned that the dinosaur's nationalized health care plan included rationed herbivorous prescription plans and the fact that Obamasaurus included secret death panels meant that he was involved with the depopulation of the Judeo-Christian Nation with his wealthy donors.

The Elders suspected that Obamasaurus intended to ration and deny treatments to Judeo-Christian dinosaurs who fell ill while exempting himself and his family and the illegals he migrated into the

Judeo-Christian Dinosaur Nation as well as his wealthy associates and donors.

The Elders believed that the Obamasaurus unread health care plan included early end-of-life counseling that would lead to assisted suicide. Dinomoses said, "It's my opinion that the Obamasaurus health care plan will result in patient dumping dinosaurs at unprecedented levels and only the wealthy will access their Cadillac health care treatments, not the eldely or the very ill. It's more about death care to the Judeo-Christian dinosaurs than health care."

The Tablets revealed that during the campaign of 2008 B.C., Obamasaurus failed to salute the Judeo-Christian Dinosaur Nation's flag or recite the Pledge of Allegiance to the Judeo-Christian Dinosaur Nation (JCDN).

Obamasaurus said, he wouldn't wear the JCDN flag on his lapel. He said the Dinosaur National Anthem was violent. He stated that the Judeo-Christian dinosaur beliefs were violent. He mocked the Judeo-Christian God. He stated that the Judeo-Christian dinosaur leaders and the Judeo-Christian Dinosaur constitutional laws were "meaningless and nothing more than a charter of negative laws that needed to be changed." Dinomoses believed that Obamasaurus was set up to bully and behave as a dictator.

Dinomoses said, "The news reported that his alleged light skin radical dinosaur grandparents and light skin radical dinosaur mom, as well as his radical light and dark skin mentors, which included the dad of his friend, a former terrorist who attacked the police and judges may have instilled a deep rooted evil opinion of the Judeo-Christians. It appears that his deep rooted resentment was taught at a very young age and created a rage deep down inside to take revenge on the Judeo-Christian Nation's dino-citizens of light to medium skin believing that harming innocent dinosaurs and persecuting and punishing or depopulating them from the planet will solve his personal inner problems that he holds onto and can't let go.

The Mad Scientist

In the meantime, the Judeo-Christian Nation wasn't aware that Dr. Fauccini was a friend of Dinogaites and Dinogeorge and the wealthy donors in the village who employed him to research and develop a new injection that could sterilize young dinosaurs and reduce the population of the sick and the elderly and the mentally and physically challenged. This was part of the depopulation program under the guise of health care that had been included in the new healthcare bill.

Dr. Fauccini was an elderly dinosaur and long-time Scientist. He was arrogant and enjoyed the attention of being in the limelight. He believed that for the better good of society that he had the right to experiment on babies, children and young people while researching a cure for a virus or an infectious disease even if the dinosaurs were injured or died. The Obamasaurus regime granted Dr. Fauccini, a Carte Blanc pass to continue even with dangerous unapproved case studies and unlicensed experimental and trial Rx drugs as well as unlicensed experimental vaccines. The entire Obamasaurus regime granted Dr. Fauccini special favor by granting him and his donors who are invested in his research a golden pass. They are granted 100% immunity from prosecution or lawsuits filed by the injured parties or the dinosaur families who lost loved ones. In fact, Dr. Fauccini was wealthy and his wealthy donors supported the agenda using experimental drugs and experimental vaccines to reduce the population of undesirable dinosaurs who they believe are no more than bottom feeders. The Obamasaurus regime allows Dr. Fauccini to use dinosaurs as Dr. Fauccini's lab rats for case studies without any liability for his part in experimental and trial medical treatments even with knowledge of unknown efficacy or consequences to individuals whether it is beneficial or permanently injures a healthy dinosaur or kills a healthy dinosaur. He and his investors have 100% immunity from all liability. That is what Elder Dinomoses refers to as gross negligence and a recipe for a potential genocide.

CHAPTER 12

Dino-Media Fake News

Shockingly, the Dino-News concealed that the new leader, Obamasaurus, spent an excessive amount of time during his youth being mentored by both dark and light skin radical dinosaurs, both domestic and foreign, who resented the Judeo-Christian Nation; capitalism, God, sovereignty, freedom, and liberty.

The dangerous ideologies of the dark skin radical dinosaurs believed it was their duty to change and transform the Judeo-Christian light to medium skin Dinosaur Nation into a melting pot and steal their nation for the infiltration of foreign enemies. The Tablets inferred that Dinomoses believed that the radical and communist dinosaurs conspired for decades against the Judeo-Christian Dinosaur Nation.

The legend stated that the Elders of the Judeo-Christian dinosaurs, who spoke out in opposition to Obamasaurus and his agendas, were discredited as conspiracy theorists. Some reporters referred to certain dinosaurs who questioned unusual sightings in the skies as dinosaurs who wore tin foil hats. Dinosaurs who insisted that the leaders uphold the vetting laws were discredited as dino-birthers. The elders were concerned about Obamasaurus and his latest experiment implemented against the dinosaurs. He mandated that the dinosaurs be radiated by forcing them into the sun without protection which can cause sterility, cancer or death if overdone.

After the climate change increased the temperatures, the sun emitted burning rays as if a microwave was placed over the sun and intensified heat. Dinojob said that he read in the dino-medical journals that there weren't any safe levels of radiation, especially for light skin dinosaurs. Over exposure to radiation from the sun can cause injury or death.

Dinomoses said, "Well, the dino-news reported that Obamasaurus is supported by thousands of members who belong to the dinosaur teachers union, SUE. Remember, Obamasaurus stated that his alleged foreign-born dark skin dinosaur dad resented the Judeo-Christian colonization of his foreign birthplace where he resided, which may have been the key that created his dinosaur dad's extreme resentment towards the Judeo-Christian Dinosaur Nation. Sheriff Joe said, "It's hard to believe that a dinosaur kid, who only saw his alleged real dinosaur dad one time during his lifetime, could know what he was thinking and what he felt or what resentments he held. It's not likely that a dinosaur kid carried those resentments for an entire lifetime after meeting his dinosaur dad once during his youth. It's reported that Obamasaurus, sr. returned to Kenyaville and died in a drunken accident.

"Everyone knows that it takes time to bond even with one's own dinosaur kids. The odds of Obamasaurus sr. influencing Obamasaurus that much over one visit is slim and none. There had to be other influences that caused him to believe the stories about the Judeo-Christian dinosaur citizens that caused such deep resentment upon an entire nation," Sheriff Dinojoe stated.

Dinojob spoke up and said, "Maybe, he suffered a lifetime of physical and emotional pain."

Dinomoses remarked, "The story of Obamasaurus or Dinobari is ridiculous. How could any rational dinosaurs possibly have bought into such a fairytale?"

Sheriff Dinojoe said, "This mysterious dinosaur, who calls himself Obamasaurus and Dinobari threatens the very existence of our Judeo-Christian foundation and its survival and that of the entire population of Judeo-Christian dinosaurs. As they say, one dinosaur can make a positive difference. Or, one dinosaur can destroy an entire nation. Too bad we let him slip in without vetting."

Dinojob paused and frowned. He said, "Public servants that we've elected have granted Obamasaurus unprecedented authority over our Judeo-Christian Dinosaur Nation and they have refused to perform their duty and uphold their sworn oath and properly vet him. We don't even know his true identity. If the masses don't wake up soon, I predict there will be unbearable suffering in the future. The storm is coming."

In the meantime, the unidentified dino-czars, who work around the clock on their agendas, secretly slipped new mandates into law and mandated same-sex education into the nation's volunteer army. Instead of the Dinosaur National Civilian Security Force guarding the borders, the security force received orders to guard Obamasaurus and keep the Judeo-Christian citizens away from him or else face arrest. The dinosaurs were witnessing freedom of religion denied when they were notified that pro-life dinosaurs were arrested for praying on public sidewalks which was very disturbing to the dinosaur citizens. The elders of the Judeo-Christian Dinosaur Nation were extremely upset and attempted to fight back, but the majority of dinosaurs feared speaking out. In fact, they arrested a Judeo-Christian dinosaur Pastor for preaching in public. He asked the question to those in attendance. If same-sex is natural then why do they have to force a sexual preference on the majority of dinosaur adults and children? Anything that is natural never needs to be forced on anyone. And, the dino-cops arrested him for speaking out. We are seeing these tyrants shut down Freedom of Speech, Religion, and Free Will and Choice.

Of course, dinosaur teachers feared losing their jobs and they feared punishment by the dinosaur SUE union. The dinosaur teachers would sit around the lunch table each day and grumble. One of the shy teachers named Dinakim said, "I don't want to teach same-sex lifestyles to dino-kids." She said, "It appears that our leaders want to control our bodies, kids, sexual decisions, and our bedrooms. This is sick and sinister to me!"

Another teacher named, Dinasarah asked, the question, "Well, if unborn dinosaur babies aren't alive at conception or afterwards then why do they have to be killed by an abortionist? Anything that isn't alive doesn't need to be killed, right?" The liberal dinosaur union members who supported Obamasaurus didn't have an answer to the question so they didn't say anything. They just looked befuddled.

Dinojay, a prominent dinosaur lawyer spoke out and remarked, "I can't believe our own Judeo-Christian dino-cops have arrested pastors and pro-life priests based on accusation only. They were arrested because foreign immigrants stated they were offended by Christian prayers. Dinofrank says, "Killing millions of unborn baby dinosaurs under the guise of abortion is nothing more than a silent genocide."

The Tablets mentioned that the elders were worried about the dinosaur youth, who were mandated to fight wars on anti-Judeo-Christian soil, but under the policies ordered by Obamasaurus, statistics reported a 70% increase of dinosaur soldiers dying on the battlefields since Obamasaurus took office. And suicides doubled on the battlefields. So, are Judeo-Christian dinosaurs being sacrificed on abortion tables, battlefields and by starvation for a cult?"

The magnificent Obamasaurus appeared as an eloquent speaker on stage and quite charming. The female dinosaurs were enamored with his smile and style. Although, he appeared thug-like at times, the females didn't seem to mind. In fact, they ignored that fact. It didn't matter what questions he was asked about his actions or his personal information, he always managed to circumvent the questions with a joke and make the audience laugh so that the questions were soon forgotten and he could move on. He announced that soon everyone must undergo a full body naked x-rayed or patted down prior to leaving the village or coming back in. The dino-citizens were very upset over his announcement.

One day, Obamasurus mentioned to the dino-reporters that he was traveling to Kenyaville and meet with their leaders about population control and implementing same-sex agendas and setting up abortion clinics funded by the Judeo-Chrstian Nation. The news reported that the leaders of Kenyaville did consider the abortion clinics, but the dino-citizens booed his same-sex indoctrination in their school system and protesters held up signs that said, "Go back to the Judeo-Christian

Nation." The Elders weren't blinded by Obamasaurus or dinogaites and dinogeorge and their members of the secret societies with their so-called save the planet agendas misrepresenting that they were concerned about saving dino-lives when they were all about wiping out dino-lives who believed in God and procreation.

Many dinosaurs accepted the idea of transformation but were misled and didn't understand that it created ideologies that would end their way of life and reduce their population and eventually wipe them off the face of the map and conquer their entire nation.

Redistribution of Food

The Redistribution of Wealth to the government and the wealthy was one of the most dangerous programs that the dinosaurs were facing. They needed to organize and unite if they were to resist the Obamasaurus mandates and demand that he resign from office. The Elders explained to those who would listen that who controls the water and the food chain controls the citizens and the prices which can be made unaffordable. Obamasaurus and dinogaites and dinogeorge intended that the appointed committee would determine who lives and who is euthanized and who is rationed or denied health care treatments or herbal medicines.

These wealthy people who appeared to be controlling everything Obamasaurus mandated. They secretly approved a mandate allowing the medical professionals to use the dinosaurs for their experiments and trials of new medical treatments and herbal medicines without knowing the consequences to each individual dinosaur or explaining the risks or obtaining consent. This was very troublesome to every Judeo-Christian dinosaur to think that their leaders were taking them hostage and using them as lab rats for experiments.

Dinomoses was very disturbed that the Judeo-Christian doctors and nurses would agree to euthanize the elderly as well as the sick or mentally challenged by denying food and water and just let the patients starve to death. These death panels were set up as appearing to be benevolent acts of kindness, but the Elders knew they were depopulation programs.

Noah recalled when a doctor that was nicknamed, Dr. Death, was illegally euthanizing the sick and elderly in America and no one stopped him. He killed many people before the courts intervened and ended his chemical-laden injections that caused an early-end-of life death.

Noah recalled another case years ago when a young girl was admitted to a hospital after a car accident that caused a coma The parents wanted to keep her alive because she was responsive to them and they wanted to take her home and care for her, but the ex-husband who was married to another woman with kids hired a lawyer and the judge sided with the ex-husband to pull the feeding tube and starve her to death in the USA which is shocking to this day.

It appeared to Noah that that these agendas reported in the news may have been the beginning of the end times by conditioning people to accept them in a Judeo-Christian Nation as beneficial. The wealthy members of secret societies believe decisions involving patient care should be made by the hospitals, judges, and government, not by the immediate family.

In fact, one wealthy man supports and donates to enforce the death panels that ration and deny health care and provide early-end-of-life counseling convincing people to be euthanized or pull the plug early on their loved ones or starve them to death if the patient is in a coma. He stated that if hospitals can make the decision to euthanize the elderly, very ill, and coma patients that the government could save millions of dollars and use that money for education.

The Tablets revealed that the dino-czars began demanding that the dino-workers must pay-up-front by ordering the Judeo-Christian dinosaurs to turn additional supplies of wealth in the form of food and water supplies over to the government. The Judeo-Christian dinosaur citizens were ending up with rationed or denied health care treatments and medicinal herbs. The food and water was being rationed. The health and lifespan of the Judeo-Christian Dinosaurs felt threatened. They were worried because they heard that the Femasaurus camps stored large ovens and no one was seen again who were forced into the camps.

Ironically, Obamasaurus' assistant, Dinanancy was more concerned about saving a few fish in the water supply that flowed on the dino-farmers land used to grow crops and herbs that needed the water supply to feed the nation. She didn't care. Dinanancy shut down the water supply to the bread basket in order to save a few fish. The farmer's crops were destroyed. The Farmers lost their livelihood. This was an inhumane and cruel thing to do to the farmers and their families and workers. The failure of the dino-citizens to act and remove Dinanancy from her position caused her to believe she was not only powerful, but untouchable.

Eventually, the dinosaur farmers ended up losing their crops and they felt betrayed and concerned over the rationing of food and water. They were now experiencing shortages of food and water ordered by the Obamasaurus mandates. The dinosaurs knew that lack of nutrition and healthy herbs and fruits and vegetables would lead to illness and diseases and eventually death if they can't farm and access food, vegetables, fruits, herbs and water.

The Judeo-Christian dinosaurs began living in fear. They knew they had to have a supply of food and water to get through droughts and freezing cold weather. They feared that they couldn't protect their dino-kids from starving to death. The Obamasaurus National Security Dinosaur Force wouldn't allow them to leave the village to gather food and water for their families. They were locked down. And, they were only allowed to have a 30 day supply of food on hand because Obamasaurus announced he would have his army knocking on their doors to search their homes and if they violated his Mandates, which were all illegal acts by Obamasaurus, but what could they do? It was illegal for Obamasaurus to use their resources to turn on the dino-citizens and remove them from their homes and be taken to Femasaurus camps until they complied and obeyed with his tyrannical mandates or perhaps, never return home again.

OBAMASAURUS PROMISED 350,000 SHOVEL-READY JOBS

Obamasaurus and Dinojb promised 350,000 shovel ready jobs to get the economy back on track and put the dinosaurs back to work so they could get their villages and farms up and running, but he lied to the Judeo-Christian Nation of Dinosaurs and easily tricked them because they trusted him. They liked him when they elected him into office. They were shocked and they didn't know what to do to stop the injustices that were being implemented in their nation that was once free. The reset of changing and transforming their nation involved death and destruction, deception, lies, and depopulation it did appear to the Elders.

Infrastructure repairs were long over due in their nation. The idea felt enticing to the dinosaur citizens who believed that they needed to restore or rebuild the infrastructure so that they wouldn't suffer severe damage from earthquakes or floods. They weren't too concerned about tornadoes or hurricanes. The dinosaurs felt safe in a rock solid cave where they could survive. On the other hand, the dinosaurs were concerned about any damage to the plants and trees as well as the fields of herbs and fruits. After the Elders gathered together, they didn't appear to be impressed with the "Chicken Little" story and fear mongering that Obamasaurus recited from his lips every time they moved. Dinomoses and Sheriff Dinojoe were wise dinosaurs and they believed that the new charismatic dinosaur in town may have other plans.

They didn't believe it was a good idea to hand over their stock piles of tools to Obamasaurus. He promised to create jobs and build safe damns and bridges, which would create a path, when traveling from village to village. This story reminded Noah of the yellow brick road in the story of the "Wizard of Oz."

CHAPTER 13

Dinodon Fights Back for Freedom

According to the ancient dinosaur Tablets, Noah noted that the Elder warned the dino-youth that one dinosaur can make a difference and that difference can be for good or evil in the world and that's why it's important to never give up in the fight for good versus evil. It is a spiritual battle that began with Dino and Dina. The good will always fight back for their unalienable God-given right to Freedom while the evil ones will do everything in their power to destroy all of God's creations upon the earth, not just Judeo-Christian dinosaurs and other species in the future, but everything that is beautiful. The Sun. The Moon. The Stars. The Oxygen. The soil. The animals. The Bugs. The Bees. The Plants. The Trees. Oceans. Rivers. Lakes. Everything the evil ones touch will be contaminated including the minds of those they influence.

The Tablets provided insight into the thoughts of the Judeo-Christians who stayed the course and stated that Satan's time is short. He is pure evil and that's why God cast him out of the Sacred Gardens. God's creations are in trouble when they believe the Scientists over God's Commandments and messages.

They are in trouble when they Trust in Scientists and no longer "Trust in God." Once, they allow fear to control their minds then the evil one thrives and uses those he made wealthy. He seeks to control as many weak minds as possible so that he can recruit by targeting the minds of the youth.

The Internet of Bodies

The evil one controls their minds until they begin to mock God and violate God's 10 Commandments by seducing them with titles, fame, wealth, land, and the material world through the televisaurus. Those who sell their souls to Satan can never enter the Kingdom of God when their soul transitions into the next life once their time and testing on earth is completed. That is why God granted everyone a Free Will and Freedom to Choose. He will not force anyone to choose God; however, He provides mercy and forgiveness for those that awaken to the truth and return to the light.

Noah's wheels were turning. He recalled reading about a new technology into the future that can be injected into the bodies of every human on the planet. It hooks the mind of every person injected with the microchips who sold their souls in exchange for wealth. The evil ones take control over their minds and bodies God created. They intend to use a therapy never used on humans as an experiment on humanity known as mRNA and Trade Secret Formula so that the government and the public won't know what else is injected into their bodies with intent to change surviving humans into mindless zombies without human emotions or thoughts.

Noah thought that the evil ones must be planning to illegally, unlawfully, and unconstitutionally mandate the FDA approved Experimental and Trial Injections because vaccines must be approved and licensed as vaccines by the FDA to be a vaccine. Otherwise, they remain an experiment and a trial and everyone injected is a human lab rat whether by fear mongering, threats, and coercion or rewards which is coercion and illegal and crimes in the USA.

Noah wondered if it was possible that the evil agenda could be to bypass the 5 year and up to 25 years of case studies for approval of efficacy and safety because too many people might wake up and begin questioning these agendas that ration and deny food and water and medicine and health care to Americans.

This haunted the mind of Noah when he recalls coming across an article in a Sci-fi magazine that intrigued him. The article was written as Sci-Fi about secret societies of wealthy people creating a world of trans humans and same sex persons only to stop procreation and reduce the population of the planet.

He recalled that the title of the Sci-fi article was called, "The Internet of Bodies" and just the title caught his attention. He wanted to know more about this Sci-fi futuristic program, so he read it and believed it to be fictional and dangerous to mankind if such a program was ever developed and rolled out.

The fictional story read that the government, who was funded by wealthy Wall Street Billionaires and CEO's of major corporations, would create a pandemic that would cause fear. so people believed they were going to die if they got the flu. This would provide the secret societies who fund the Health Care and key politicians an opportunity to use their puppet government officials to mandate FDA experimental and trial injections and bypass the 5 year up to 25 year case studies that are needed to be approved for a "licensed vaccine"

In this fictional Sci-fi story, they knew this experimental and trial injection would pass them by if they waited 5 years or more and they would lose their opportunity and their investment into this program, so they convinced the key persons in positions of power to call out lockdowns and mandates. They fear mongered, threatened, and coerced the population to be injected if they wanted to go back to work or school and socialize. They also threatened those who resisted that they would be isolated like lepers from society and fired from their jobs and impoverished and isolated. How is that part of health care?

The wealthy people involved in this Sci-fi fictional story knew that they needed a built-in customer base for-profit and a built-in free population of Human Lab Rats with knowledge that millions might die in the future or healthy people might be mentally or physically disabled. But, after all the animal Lab Rats died after 2 jabs, they needed human lab rats to inject and monitor and control for the worldwide FDA approved experimental and trial injections. The end goal is hooking up the minds and bodies to the internet, where these evil ones who sold out their souls for the material world can change and alter the God-given DNA of God's human creation and sterilize them. It is possible they could erase religion and God and conservatism. What if Scientists used advanced RFID chips to erase God, Religion and conservatism from the minds of human beings with intent to change and enslave humanity turning people into mindless zombies by injection or RFID chips?

Noah believed that was the most bothersome Sci-fi futuristic article that he ever read and the most dangerous to even conceive that anyone would carry out such an evil program which would equate to Crimes against Humanity and violations of the Nuremberg Codes and violations of the U.S. Constitution that prohibits slavery and servitude as well as using people as chattel and property to do with what they please. It bothered Noah because throughout history, psychiatrists and Mad Scientists and people who take bribes used experimental and trial injections and surgeries and mind control on people inside psychiatric wards, government schools and prisons and even the military troops. Indonesians. Blacks. Jews. Christians. And minorities have suffered from psychopaths who gain positions of power and agree to fund and support Crimes against Humanity and violations of Nuremberg Codes.

Suddenly, Noah realized he needed to get back to the Tablets as time was running out. Dinomoses liked the wealthy tycoon named Dinodon who remained neutral over the years as he was a builder and enjoyed developing a better world for the dinosaurs. He wasn't a politician, so he remained neutral so he could get their cooperation when he came up with new ideas, especially on infrastructure so they wouldn't be devastated by mudslides or drought. Dinodon believed their village needed to build a wall and keep their nation safe and secure from outside unknown species who may do harm, but Dinomoses wondered if Dinodon was too late to save the Judeo-Christian Dinosaur Nation from Obamasaurus and Dinojb.

Dinomoses warned that the reptilian dinosaurs made some sort of new tool that could behead dinosaurs swiftly. He said, "I think they are called guillotines.

They are secretly stored inside the Femasaurus camps." Dinogaites, a wealthy business owner was respected within the dinosaur nation for his inventions, but few were aware that he supported the use of guillotines for organ harvesting and depopulation programs. The Elders feared that the youth was being led away from God's Commandment that one dinoman and one dinowoman should marry and fill the earth with their species as all species were created to do so they could survive and thrive upon the earth for generations. The Judeo-Christian nation was attempting to find a way to save their civilization and their fellow dino-citizens and take back their nation, but were at a loss on how to avoid the punishments mandated by Obamasaurus so they met in secret.

Noah took a break and drank some water from his canteen. He didn't know why, but the name Jim Jones, popped into his head. He couldn't help but think how the dinosaur's fear of depopulation was similar to the agenda of Jim Jones. He recalled reading in the newspaper when a stranger came into the town of a suburban neighborhood and set up a church. He targeted an upper middle-class area and gave himself a title. He called himself a Pastor. He was handsome. Tall. Charismatic. He presented himself as a prophet and a pastor who would take care of the lost sheep. He slowly began hinting that the End Times were coming to America. He suggested that his followers sell everything and turn over all their assets and money to him. He convinced his victims to jet off to a remote land in Africa where they could live free and safe and grow their own organic foods. This was similar to the Hippie movement of the 1960s. The young adults and even some mature adults found themselves mesmerized by the new stranger in town.

The young and mature women were attracted to Jim Jones soft voice and charm. Many young females are insecure, but he made them feel good about themselves. Men and women and children followed his teachings and although he never properly identified himself and no one bothered to do a background check or ask for identification, they sold all their assets and gave their money to Jim Jones. As it turned out, he was no more than a professional broke con artist. He founded a cult in the USA misleading his followers to believe he was the messiah and just like Obamasaurus made false promises, so history does repeat itself.

Eventually, Jones and his civilian army and followers moved to a foreign land. After Jones learned the government was investigating his identity and his sudden wealth, he didn't want any witnesses around, so apparently, there were followers who wanted to go back to America, but they weren't allowed to leave.

They were held hostage against their will it appears. He learned that a U.S. member of Congress was flying in to investigate his cult. Jones was prepared.

The leader ordered his army to kill the member of Congress before he was able to get on the plane safely. The leader then ordered his armed thugs to hold the American men, women, and children hostage in the camp at gun point. He forced them to drink the Kool-Aid under threat of being executed. The members drank the poisoned Kool-Aid. There were only a few survivors who managed to play dead. Noah thought, this is how easily people are tricked and how easily a small or a large genocide of a few innocent people or millions of innocent people are depopulated and their deaths become "meaningless" as people forget.

Noah wondered if the elders and wealthy owner, Dinodon, came too late to rescue the Judeo-Christian Nation's dinosaurs from the treasonous acts being implemented against their nation and the potential genocide as well as a potential to force survivors into barbed wire Femasaurus camps.

Noah continued to read the Judeo-Christian Dinosaur Tablets. He felt as if he was experiencing a rude awakening and wondered if it was possible that wealthy men could conspire worldwide to wipe out the majority of humanity and conquer the United States of America and eliminate God's existence from the planet. After all, Lucifer works overtime to mock God and uses people to seduce them to buy into the material world.

The Tablets revealed that the Elders were disturbed when they heard that Obamasaurus was approving new laws that punished the dinosaur whistleblowers who warned of the infiltration of foreign anti-Judeo-

Christian radical dinosaurs being secretly migrated into their country at night and scattered around the nation.

The Elders began hearing rumors that witnesses and whistleblowers were in the news of suddenly dying from accidents and heart attacks and they felt that was very strange, indeed. Dinomoses felt it was time to plan an exodus for the Judeo-Christian heterosexuals who appeared to be the target in his mind as part of the Obamasaurus, Dinogaites and Dinogeorge depopulation agendas. He and the Elders began a secret search for a safe place that would be extremely difficult to locate where they could be safe. He prayed for God to show him the way.

He believed that it was their duty to tell the history so that future generations will be informed of the super powerful dinosaurs who developed the Judeo-Christian Dinosaur Nation that was seduced by one foreign radicalized and non-vetted reptilian magnificent and charismatic dinosaur who won the hearts of the youth. The leaders of the Judeo-Christian Dinosaur Nation refused to follow the Rule-of-Law and perform their duty. They failed to vet or identify Obamasaurus upon entry into their nation. They failed to vet his credentials even after he applied to be the leader of their sovereign nation.

Consequently, fear was the greatest enemy facing the Judeo-Christian Nation of peaceful and God-fearing dinosaurs. The majority of Judeo-Christian dinosaur citizens were sorry that they didn't ask Obamasaurus, "Who are you and can you prove who you really are — Dinobari or Obamasaurus?

Obamasaurus declared that he would Rule the Judeo-Christian nation without the Elders and without their "Ten Commandments. He stated he would write his own laws which he referred to as the Obamasaurus Executive Order Mandates. It appears that Obamasaurus appeared to have a goal. He's wasn't flexible in his thinking and he had tunnel vision because of his childhood and because he was on a mission. He believed that he would be the One World Order dictator and transform the world according to his vision which meant Judeo-Chrsitians or Patriots, who opposed his agendas would be punished. Everyone was to worship Obamasaurus. Pray to him. Sing Praises of him. Acknowledge him as the messiah. He sought to Rule under a One World Government, One World Leader, and One World Religion using an iron fist.

One of the dino-czars, Dinocary attended a meeting with the Elders and arrogantly reminded them that he and his peers believed that the Elders are from the old school with old ideas because they are old fashion and they're stuck in their traditions and their beliefs of God and Judeo-Christian laws." The Elders were not shocked but were worried knowing that Dinocary was in for a rude awakening down the road and he was selling out his soul for the material world.

Dinocary blurted out, "We're young. We're from the new school. We have new ideas that demand change, not your old traditions." The younger generation of dinosaurs didn't care if Obamasaurus didn't prove that he was a natural-born citizen and wasn't vetted properly or that he made their laws meaningless. They only cared about him being hip and cool and youthful.

Dinobari was a fabulous new Rock Star in their eyes, but now all of the dino-youth fell for it. But, those that did were caught up in the glitz and glitter and false promises that Obamasaurus would take care of the necessities of life. They believed what they wanted to believe and heard what they wanted to hear. They weren't told the other side of the story that he intended to change and replace them with foreign anti-Judeo-Christians, which is their written and stated strategic goal to wipe out the Judeo-Christian Dinosaur Nation and dominate and conquer their Homeland.

Dinomoses said, "Without justice, vetting, equality, fairness, and 'Due Process of Law,' there will be nothing but tyranny." Dinomoses was exhausted from fighting back against the pending evil agendas without media support. As Noah continued reading the Tablets, he learned that time was running out for the Elders who worked tirelessly to save their Judeo-Christian Dinosaur Nation.

The legend stated that sadness fell upon the room of Elders and resonated like the sound of music." He learned that the Elders felt weary and they were running out of creative ideas to save the nation.

Dinodon was present and stated, "We must save the Judeo-Christian Dinosaur Nation." We must never give up. We must make our nation great again. There are infiltrators inside our nation. They are Deep State enemies of God who worship the false golden idol that dwells deep down underneath the ground where they meet and plan to do harm and evil to those who are not one of them. We must fight back against evil, but the Elders felt they must move on now as they had little time left.

The Elders spoke about planning an exodus to escape from the tyrannical laws under the Obamasaurus regime. The Judeo-Christian dinosaur citizens feared that it would be too late for the dinosaurs to begin an exodus. They also realized that millions of Judeo-Christian dinosaurs could end up on a secret hit list or they could be indefinitely detained in the Femasaurus camps or assassinated if the winds blew in an ugly direction. After all, Obamasaurus and Dinogaites were tracking and spying on every Judeo-Christian in the nation with the secret army of recruits who joined the National Civilian Security Dino-Force.

Dinoeric, who worked for Obamasaurus stated to the Judeo-Christian school kids that the Judeo-Christian Dinosaur citizens would be polarized because within a matter of years, the face of the Judeo-Christian Dinosaur Nation would be changed forever. His statement upset the Elders and the citizens who heard about his comment. And, it was rumored that wealthy Dinogaites requested a secret study on Dinosaur Commodities for Dinosaur Capital for the wealthy dinosaurs who were seeking to determine the worth or lack of worth of each Judeo-Christian dinosaur.

The legend read that a few minutes later, Dinojob stated, "Look, if God had intended for the earth to be void of baby dinosaurs, he wouldn't have created one male and one female dinosaur for procreation. He wouldn't have commanded Dino and Dina to get married and bond and be fruitful by birthing baby-dinosaurs upon the earth. He would have made the female dinosaurs sterile so they couldn't conceive baby dinosaurs. They watched the televisaurus when the wealthy Dinogaites stated in a dino-press interview that if they could euthanize the elderly and the sick and mentally and physically challenged that they would save tons of food and water and use it to educate the youth. Dinogaites believes there are too many dinosaurs on the earth. How is it that no one is paying attention to these domestic enemy radicals?"

Dinomoses said, "Yes, we know that the only way to preserve a nation of laws, traditions, and natural-born Judeo-Christian dinosaurs is for a male and female to bond and procreate and bring future generations of natural-born babies into the nation in order for them to be taught to love our nation and grow up and preserve our nation and our Homeland in the future through procreation. It's the natural-born citizens who preserve sovereign nations. God knows everyone will die and that the only way to preserve nations is to give birth to more natural-born citizens, otherwise the nation's history and civilization will be changed and wiped off the face of the map forever."

Dinojob said, "It's clear that the dinosaur Framers included Article II as an established Rule of Law in order to preserve the Judeo-Christian Dinosaur Nation for future generations. Only a baby dinosaur born on the Judeo-Christian Dinosaur Nation's soil to 2 natural-born dinosaur parents is eligible to be the leader of the Judeo-Christian Nations. It is the greatest privilege and honor bestowed upon the natural-born citizen. Why would the Judeo-Christian natural-born dino-youth even consider giving away the only law that separates them and honors them to be the only ones to lead their great Republic and protect their sovereignty and fellow Judeo-Christian citizens from being invaded and conquered?

The Natural Born Citizen's Privilege and Honor

Dinodon stated, "It's clear that our Framers believed that only a natural born dinosaur citizen will love their country and fellow dinosaurs more than foreigners and that a natural-born citizen will work harder to preserve their nation for future generations. I was cheated out of my legal right to be the leader of the Judeo-Christian Nation. We must now ask, should we not fight back or give up?"

"The foreigner fraudulently stole the legal Birthright right to the office of President of our nation from the natural-born eligible candidate which was unprecedented in our history as Dinodon should have won the second election when Dinodon stepped out of the race," stated Dinojob.

Dinomoses said, "We did elect Dinodon, but something happened during our elections that went wrong. Dinodon could be entrusted to protect, defend and preserve the laws rooted from the Ten Commandments and the Old Testament, but instead we now face danger of extinction and the loss of our Homeland by the foreign enemies assisted by domestic enemies. Ironically, the anti-Christian foreigners don't get abortions who overpopulate which should be the other way around. Judeo-Christians should overpopulate so a strong army could defend our nation from being conquered. Obamasaurus exempted the radical foreigners from abortions and same sex and from rationed and denied healthcare, food, and water and arrests. In fact, he released all foreigners who committed crimes against the Judeo-Christian citizens from the Femasaurus camps and funded them and set them free.

The Tablet reveals that the elections were dishonest in 2008 B.C., 2012 B.C., and 2020 B.C. so that Obamasaurus and Dinojb would continue on with their agendas funded by the wealthy secret society members so that the agendas of the wealthy Wall Street secret society members could also carry on with their sinister agendas that they've invested in and seek to reap the profits in the future.

Unfortunately, the Tablets stated that the population of Judeo-Christian light to medium skin dinosaurs diminished down to the lowest ever in their history over three generations because the liberal light to medium Judeo-Christian feminist dinosaurs aborted millions of natural-born baby dinosaurs who could have helped save their nation, but now it was too late to make up for the loss as the dino-citizens faced a crisis and were facing a crossroads between life and death.

Dinomoses was very upset that the youth turned their back on God's Commandments of procreation and commanded them to obey the law that read, "Thou Shalt Not Kill." God only intended for every species to be able to defend themselves and their families from enemies who try to harm innocents or invade nations with intent of stealing their Homeland.

At this point, the reset for the Judeo-Christian Nation with fewer or no Judeo-Christians in the future was set. The wealthiest in the nation, Dinogeorge and dinogaites funded Dr. Le Fauccini and Doctor Le Emmanuel who were working hard at the wealthy owner's ranch who built a lab for the doctor and Scientist to perform their Research and Development. It was located on top of a mountain in a rural area hard to access. The wealthy owner, Dinojeff supported eugenics and abortions. He also sought to lower the age of children so adults could marry dino-kids. He funded euthanasia programs and provided funding the R&D to develop the superior race.

Of course, the dinosaur pastors of the Judeo-Christian churches spoke out in defense of protecting the lives of the the Judeo-Christian unborn baby dinosaurs, but Obamasaurus shocked the Dinosaur Nation when he approved of indefinite detention at the Femasaurus Camps for Judeo-Christians who opposed mandating the funding of abortions and forcing Judeo-Christians to participate on Judeo-Christian soil. The Judeo-Christians knew that this would offend God and that God's wrath who warned them not to harm children would fall upon their nation in God's time and in God's way.

Nonetheless, a dinosaur pastor, Dinopat, appeared on the televisaurus and stated, "Same-sex indoctrination of minor kids and schools being taught under the guise of education should be vehemently opposed by the school principals and Department of Education. The schools are ignoring parental rights and the right to exempt their dino-kids from indoctrinating minor Judeo-Christian dino-kids into their sexual preferences in violation of their religious beliefs.

The protests by the dino-parents fell on deaf ears and the only exemptions for religion was granted to the anti-Judeo-Christian foreigners whose ideologies bonded their foreign religion and law as one and the same and could not be separated.

As Noah continued to read the Tablets, the carvings indicated that Obamasaurus felt empowered by his success at changing the Judeo-Christian Dinosaur Nation with the help of some of the Judeo-Christian leaders who were taking food and water incentives in exchange for going along with Obamasaurus. In fact, no one who voted for Obamasaurus was upset even after Obamasaurus instructed them to put on their bedroom slippers and hit the streets and promote his agendas to the Judeo-Christian Dinosaur citizens by knocking on their doors.

The legend revealed that Obamasaurus shocked the dinosaur parents when he issued an order to the public schools that he intended to defund basic educational classes such as Calculus, algebra II, P.E., English, Computer Science, Art, Music, and police safety. He was inserting the teachings of a foreign anti-Judeo-Christian religion in place of these studies.

The dino-parents were shocked when Obamasaurus and Dinojb approved of incentives for same-sex education under the guise of health care that would replace Physical Ed. classes. He also informed the dino-parents that he approved using the gym to set up hubs at the schools where his medical czars could perform abortions without parental consent on the school grounds. He also stated that he would provide the kids without parental consent with the dino-herb abortion serum that could be taken on the morning after to end any possibility of a pregnancy. The notice stated that the schools would be using the gym to build hubs where they would perform abortions instead of playing sports. The dino-parents were furious.

In fact, Obamasaurus boasted of funding the installation of vending machines into every public school. The dino-parents weren't so surprised when at another one of his evil agendas informing them that the vending machines were not to be filled with snacks. They were stocked with herbal morning after serum and condoms. The dino-parents sought out Sheriff Dinojoe and Officer Dinomack and Elders Dinomoses, Dinojb and Dinodon seeking answers to these serious agendas.

The citizens feared being sent to the Femasaurus Camps or indefinitely detained or assassinated or having their kids removed from their custody for opposing or criticizing anything Obamasaurus and Dinojb enacted illegally, unlawfully or unconstitutionally, because they had wealthy and powerful anti-Judeo-Christian turncoats on their side building an army against the dino-citizens.

Noah was so intrigued by the dinosaur legend that he lost track or time. He deciphered that the Judeo-Christian Elders considered the dangers of an exodus, but felt it was the only way out now to save the children, not to save the nation.

The Elders set up a plan for an exodus from their beloved Homeland and those who chose to secretly leave while there was still time before they shut down the borders. They planned to exit their Homeland at night in groups of families, but not all at once. They discovered the secret cave on the top of the mountain with many separate caves so that each family could live together. They had a wonderful water supply.

Dinojob said, "We have no time to lose. I heard through the grapevine that Obamasaurus is planning to require papers to exit and enter at the borders."

Noah was intrigued when he read the following: On a warm summer day, the dinosaurs experienced an unprecedented storm. The storm wiped out homes, crops, and destroyed trees and plants. Many of the dinosaurs ended up homeless. Life for the dinosaurs appeared dismal. After the summer ended and the leaves turned yellow, orange, and red, the Autumn months began, the climate change flip flopped from extreme heat to extreme cold.

There wasn't any explanation for the climate change. The freezing temperatures affected the plants, trees, wild life, food, and water supplies as well as the health of the dinosaurs. Noah came across one Tablet that reveals how Dinomoses discovered that Obamasaurus and his regime were purchasing farmlands and water supplies.

Dinomoses said that it was important for the next species to remember these words. He stated, "Remember, those who control the food and water supplies can control a nation or even the world's population."

As time passed, Mr. Obamasaurus, became more tyrannical. He declared, "I am requiring every dino-citizen hand over 80% of their food and water supplies for the redistribution of wealth which will be redistributed to those who obey and comply. You must be tattooed with a number and stand in line and distance and do not touch each other. Everyone must wear a mask so that you don't kiss and limit your conversations. He said, "Remember, Silence is golden. Everyone will get use to thinking and talking and eating less food and drinking less water, but you'll be happy. You can stand in line twice per week for a bag of bread and water and vegetables and herbs. If you miss out that day then you must wait for the next day that is scheduled for you to return to obtain your survival care packages."

According to the legend, Obamasaurus was known as the most pro-abortion dinosaur on the planet. He enacted worldwide abortions of poor foreign nations. He believed that the indigent were also a burden on the planet. But, Obamasaurus and his wealthy donors were exempted from signing up or paying up or complying with the Obamasaurus health care programs. The wealthy could afford cadillac health care that was not affordable to the average Judeo-Christian dinosaur family. Obamasaurus created two classes of citizens. The wealthy and the poor and eliminated the Middle Class working dino-citizens.

He exempted his unidentified dino-czars and the schoolteachers union known as (SUE) School Union Employees. He exempted (SWU), the Still Working Union, as well as wealthy dinosaur supporters. In fact, Obamasaurus and his regime exempted the anti-Judeo-Christian foreign-born radicals he migrated into the nation under the guise of refugees, but they were not refugees, they were radical anti-Judeo-Christian foreign enemies. They didn't come to assimilate, but they came to receive all the freebies for life that Obamasaurus promised them upon arrival that included shelter, food, water, televisaurus, herbal medicine, freedom, liberty and rights that were now being denied to the Judeo-Christian natural-born citizen living on their Homeland.

The Tablets read that Obamasaurus and Dinogaites and Dinogeorge along with the Directors of (HOO) (Health Operational Org) and the (CDCEE) Cemetery, Directory, Cremation and Educational Elitist were ordered to determine the potential adverse health effects and projections of deaths after they locked down the dinosaur nation of Judeo-Christians who would be arrested and taken to Femasaurus camps if they were caught praying or singing or chanting praises to their God. If they didn't comply with his health care mandates and carry proof of their treatments as he now labeled the Judeo-Christians as domestic enemies if they failed to comply with his mandates.

The HOO and CDCEE were created to inform Obamasaurus, Dinogaites and Dinogeorge as to how many healthy farms and ranches were destroyed. Obamasaurus was buying them up below value. They were to inform them how many trees, plants, cows, pigs, goats, sheep, dogs, cats, horses and chickens were destroyed after locking down the farms owned and operated by the dino-Judeo-Christian farmers. Dinogaites and HOO and CDCEE destroyed their profits because Dinogaites and Monsinto were developing their own foods and meat that were in Research and Development in a lab operated by the famous dino-Scientist, Dr. Le Fauccini. The dinosaurs were ordered not to grow their own foods or vegetables.

Dinodon etched this evil agenda into the Tablets and he, too, joined the exodus. The dino-youth had been so brainwashed through the school system funded by Dinogaites and Dinogeorge that they feared touching each other or even their parents. The dino-kids were brainwashed that if they touched anyone that they will die or cause someone else to die. Dinodon said, "This is dino-child abuse."

The dinosaur kids had been brainwashed into living a life of isolation and masking and distancing for depopulation purposes, and the dino-parents who successfully joined the exodus were busy deprogramming the dino-kids. In fact, the indoctrination included spying on their parents and friends, so that was another dino-child abuse program implemented by Obamasaurus, Dinogaites, Dinogeorge and their wealthy associates.

Noah was getting a lesson in real life and what he read and what was happening in America and how even the universities were silencing professors on what they can or can't teach about American History or Religion. He thought in reality that tolerance of evil or anti-American ideologies is communism, not Americanism.

He recalled an incident in his classroom after he dismissed the class. He was grading papers and organizing his desk, but prior to that incident, he recalled reading in a newspaper that informed lawyers of new laws and cases. The government approved of several secret agencies setting up hot lines to provide tips anonymously that allowed an anonymous person to accuse anyone of a crime even if it was a lie without providing their name or identification. He felt that bordered on communism and spying on fellow Americans and to be a tool for abuse. He realized that if someone is accused of a crime even if 100% innocent, that they could be investigated. An accused could end up with legal fees trying to prove their innocence.

This part of the Tablet caught Noah's attention because he recalled finding a note on a student's desk that he accidentally left behind on his desk. He picked it up and was shocked. It was addressed to another student and stated that if a neighbor supports any anti-Liberal candidate that they can call social services on the anonymous tip line and accuse them of child abuse or spousal abuse and maybe, they'll get the message. Noah knew that there were government agencies who offered anonymous hot lines, but he never thought that they would be used for sinister or political agendas or pranks.

OBAMASAURUS": Raising Donations
to Build Femasaurus Camps

The dinosaurs who didn't join the exodus were indefinitely detained after the Obamasaurus and Dinojb made it it impossible to exit at the borders without showing their papers and permanent inked tattoos. Freedom, Liberty, and Rights and Sovereignty were wiped out. The dino-citizens who did join the exodus could see the Femasaurustrains from the mountain top taking the Judeo-Christian dinosaurs who resisted complying with the evil and sinister mandates implemented that Obamasaurus and Dinojb enacted.

Obamasaurus, Dinogaites and Dinogeorge and the HOO and CDCEE caused the Judeo-Christian dinosaur families to lose their income and homes as well as their jobs and businesses with their immoral and possibly illegal indefinite detentions and lock downs. They caused an increase in broken homes and suppressed the herbal cures for the flu. They enacted good dino-citizens to be arrested for praying, singing, chanting, and attending church services. They caused the food chain to be broken and destroyed Farms and caused rationing and denying of food and water and othe products. They fear mongered and threatened and coerced the dino-citizens with either punishments or rewards.

They caused the elderly and the dino-youth to become severely depressed and lonely to the point of committing suicide. They caused the loss of crops, Food Supply, Water Supply, Businesses and Jobs in the Judeo-Christian Dinosaur Nation. The Elders asked how that could be possible when they have no constitutional authority to make laws or implement or enact them that are not moral, ethical, just, and in the Best Interest of the dinosaur world.

All Judeo-Christian dinosaurs were to be micro-chipped by 2027 B.C. so that Obamasaurus and Dinogaites and Dinogeorge could spy and track and punish the dinosaurs who resisted orders and possibly send them to the guillotines stored below the Femasaurus Camps. Noah thought about Hitler and the Nazis as well as Pol Pot. Stalin. Saddam. Morsi. ISIS. Taliban. al Qaeda. and many more on foreign soil throughout history who committed genocides and conspired and premeditated mass murders up to 100,000,000 people by one evil man.

Furthermore, Noah believed that people don't realize that the biggest killers of life are the greedy wealthy CEOs who get rich spraying the skies with chemicals and contaminating the air we breathe as well as the soil and water supplies. Are the toxic oil spills into the oceans all accidents? Are radiation spills into the atmosphere and the oceans all accidents? There is an unprecedented number of wildfires in the USA burning down the trees needed for fresh oxygen and creating toxins in the atmosphere and disrupting the animal life. The fact that tornadoes and hurricanes and winds and flooding are at unprecedented numbers. The wealthy spend their money figuring out how to radiate homes through smart meters and computers, phones, laptops, and microwaves. Also, suntanning beds were regulated in salons because the government said that too much radiation is dangerous to humans; so under Obama and Biden's watch, they installed full body radiation machines in all the airports with unknown levels of radiation cooking one's body. Doctors say that the radiation sets off the free radicals that began attacking healthy cells in the body and it's irreversible and can cause cancer and death.

Dinosaurs were confounded by the failure of the dinosaur leaders, who didn't repeal and fight back for their Judeo-Christian Nation, so they were found equally guilty in the eyes of the Elders and the patriotic dinosaurs.

Sadly, the Judeo-Christian dinosaurs began suffering from post-traumatic distresses because they placed their trust in Obamasaurus and the dinosaur elected and appointed leaders. The leaders swore an oath to uphold, defend, preserve, and protect Freedom, Liberty, and Rights, but instead, they conspired with the Obamasaurus-czars. They ate the Cornhusker soup and drank the Gatorade and played games while the Judeo-Christian Dinosaurs were starving and being abused.

The natural-born dinosaurs turned on their own citizens and were seduced by incentives. They became domestic enemies of the Judeo-Christians and traitors to their nation. They made secret backroom deals and offered foreign enemies bribes for votes. They supported violations of law through the Open Border Policies.

Unfortunately, the dinosaurs learned the hard way that a passive species were rendered helpless and ended up at the mercy of foreign and domestic enemies who conspired to overthrow their nation by refusing to uphold the laws. The law requires proper identification and background checks so a foreign enemy doesn't infiltrate into the highest office in the land. They were passive and the Elders who complained that they must vet Obamasaurus were mocked by the dino-press and labeled as "birthers" and "ignorant" and "intolerant" and "politically incorrect."

Noah was tired and he dreaded walking back to camp, but he didn't have a choice. He wasn't physically exhausted, but mentally exhausted. The Tablets gave him more information than he had ever really thought about when he read the newspaper. In the past, he didn't think about the dangers that threatened the preservation of "The Constitution of the United States of America."

He now realized how important state and federal laws establishing immigration and legal entry, legal vetting, legal applications, and legal identification by Border Patrol, ICE, and Sheriffs mattered. In the end, Sheriff DinoJoe was correct that illegal immigration is illegal and leaves Americans vulnerable to foreign enemies, criminals, traffickers, drugs, guns, and threatens the very safety and welfare of every natural-born American who isn't pro-active and paying attention.

As he gathered up his belongings, he thought it was important that all illegals and all fake refugees and all foreign enemies who didn't show up for their court dates and didn't wait in line behind the foreigners who applied legally should not be given a pass to cheat and force their way into the front of the line. Thousands have waited to become legal naturalized citizens of the USA and anxious to call themselves "Americans" and assimilate as Americans. Noah felt good that the only persons that can't be deported from America are natural-born Americans. He now realized that even legal naturalized Americans can be deported if they commit crimes against America and the Constitution as long as we fight back to preserve "The U.S. Constitution" and the Republic operated by the Rule of Law.

Noah's head was exploding. but in a good way. He yawned and stretched then grabbed his backpack and walked back down the mountainside to his campsite. His eyes felt heavy from reading and he needed to rest his bloodshot and tired eyes. After he reached the campsite, he was exhausted. He laid down on the cot and grabbed a small bottle of eyedrops and refreshed his eyes before he closed them and fell into a deep sleep. The next morning, Noah washed up and dressed. He brewed a pot of coffee and looked over his notes while he fried 2 eggs and bacon. He packed 2 sandwiches and a variety of fruit and drinks because this would be his last trek up the mountain trail. It was a beautiful day.

The sun was shining through the lush tropical trees and the birds were chirping and he felt great.

Noah realized that he couldn't reveal everything he saw or heard or read because the average person will never experience seeing a strange object in the sky or taste fruit as sweet as sugar picked off the trees in this remote jungle.

They would never believe a story about Dr. Lee or the Dinosaur Tablets etched in stone by symbols. He would keep those secrets to himself. He also realized that millions of people won't agree with his assessment on abortion, sovereignty, and resisting fear mongering over being used for experiments and trials as human lab rats.

Noah ate a hearty breakfast and afterwards, while packing up, he mumbled, "My friends would say - Noah, you need another vacation or else you need to visit a psych," if Noah even dared to share what he experienced."

The moment of truth hit Noah. He now believed that only a minority of people are chosen to see unidentified objects in the sky or hear strange noises in the skies or underground that aren't normal to see or hear or experience. He felt Blessed to be chosen for this mission. Most people wouldn't recognize strange lights or sightings in the sky. He believed that most people would dismiss it or ignore what they see and move on. Noah wondered if this must be the reason people are chosen to discover something extraordinary or experience the mysteries of this planet and the universe even if it's just a tiny piece of the puzzle for people who seek knowledge.

He looked down after he finished eating and packing up and decided to jot down his thoughts, "Although, people who experience something out of the ordinary are viewed as "crazies" or "conspiracy theorists," the truth is that even the Scientist don't know much about the universe because the universe is so vast and endless and time doesn't stand still for anyone.

The world is consistently and constantly changing. Each person is here for a short time and some people experience a simple life and believe only in what they can see or hear, taste or smell, while others are chosen or blessed to experience what the majority will never see or hear or taste or smell or believe. It is true that everyone is unique and everyone's experience upon the earth is unique." Noah believed that another message for him to share is to fight back for "Freedom of Speech" and never let any taxpayer funded director or leader silence Americans or any media entity or social media giant silence Americans.

Noah said aloud, "I think I have a better appreciation for life and animals." He thought about the animals. Bees. Fish. Mammals. Turtles. Birds. Plants. Trees. Water. Fresh Air. And, first and foremost, more love for God. He softly said, "Only God could have created such beauty upon the earth. He paused. How little we know about the wonderful world we live in and places never touched or seen by human beings that God created for us to explore. God created a mind so we can expand our horizons and seek knowledge."

In fact, it crossed Noah's mind that maybe babies and children in America should be placed on an endangered species list. After all, 100s of 1000s go missing every year and millions are wiped out at Planned Parenthood. If we can save the animal world then why can't we save the babies and the children?"

Noah felt sad that his journey was coming to an end. He felt as if he learned more on his journey than any book could ever reveal to him about the mysteries of life that most people never experienced. He felt that we must have a strong instinct even as kids. Life is filled with mysteries, but how is it only a few investigate?

He thought, people really do need to demand psychiatric evaluations of candidates for President and Vice President as well as for Congress. Why should so few people have the power to save lives or wipe out millions of lives and without oversight plot to exterminate tribes or commit a genocide that could kill millions of species and human beings? Wipe them off the face of the map.

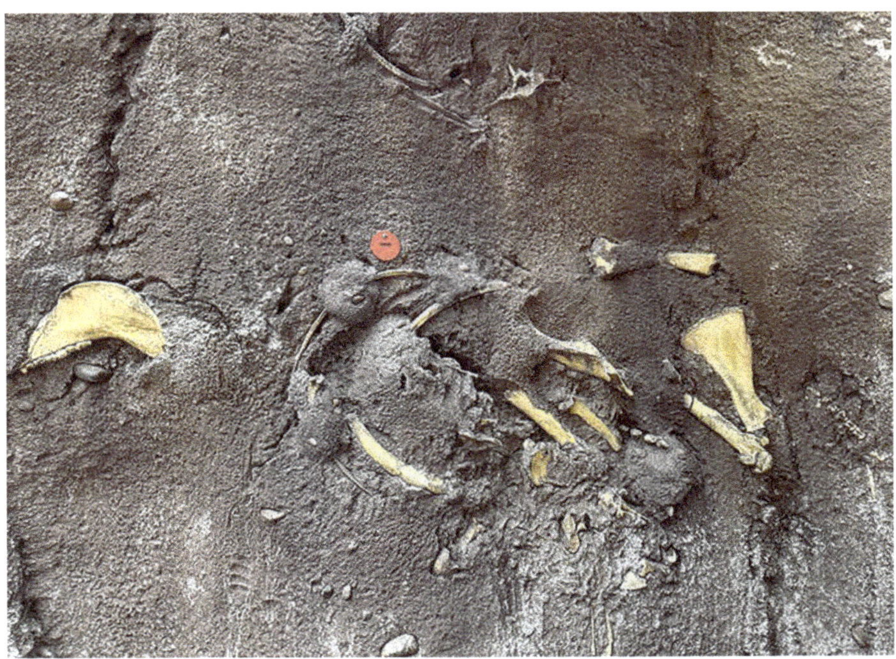

Noah wandered some more through the cave because he wanted to remember if there were other rooms inside the cave that the heterosexual dinosaurs enjoy, and he saw openings. He didn't know how deep the cave extended, but it appears to be quite vast, and he wouldn't dare explore any further by himself.

He saw one area where plants and herbs and fruit trees thrived and grew tall and healthy in a specific area where the sunlight and the rain could reach the trees and plants, so he believed they had figured out a way to have not only water, but food. Noah believed they were preppers and survivors led by Dinomoses to safety. Noah was amazed.

Stop Show Your Papers!

CHAPTER 14

Stop Freedom: Depopulation

The legend indicated that Dinomoses fought to the end against the mandated abortion program, but to no avail. The new health care mandates required an evaluation of every pregnant dinosaur by the The Psychiatrist, Dr. Emmanuel Le Reptilian, promoted eugenics. He approved of euthanizing the elderly and the very sick. The reptilian psychiatrist would present his psychiatric evaluations of the "Committee of 9" so they could determine who gives birth and which unborn baby dinosaurs would be aborted.

Of course, there wasn't any reason to worry if a botched abortion occurred. The staff sought the assistance from the Department Chair, Dr. Emanuel Le Reptilian. He would send for his medical staff, which included, Dr. Puff, which was a nickname given to him, because in one big puff, he'd snuff out the unborn baby dinosaurs before they took their first breath outside of the womb. Noah took away from this revelation of the Tablets that he believed all people should have the right to control their own bodies and minds. He now believed in downsizing the federal government and eliminating agencies too big to control. The citizens should be informed of their leader's true agendas of each Director and who donates to these agencies. What influence are they insisting upon so that their agendas are carried out without transparency and public scrutiny and for public review without being silenced by city or county or state elected officials. They dismiss the Will of the majority of Americans and dismiss them as insignificant and their input as "meaningless."

Noah felt we must get Big Brother and AI out of our bedrooms, churches, schools, colleges and universities and get back to basic Rule of Law for all, not some.

Obamasaurus Indulges Freely! Orders Rationing of Food and Water for the Judeo-Christian Dinosaur Nation

In the meantime, Obamasaurus continued to redistribute the wealth of the Judeo-Christian Dinosaur Nation to anti-Judeo-Christian dinosaur nations. This obsession to send excessive redistribution of wealth to foreign enemy nations threatening to wipe out the Judeo-Christian Dinosaur Nation off the face of the map. The intent to dominate and conquer the Judeo-Christian Nation continued against opposition by the Judeo-Christian dino-citizens who resisted these sinister agendas. They continued to protest against the open borders where unidentified anti-Judeo-Christian foreigners were pouring into the nation by the millions.

Dinodon never gave up trying to keep the dino-citizens who joined the exodus united and uplifted declaring that God would intervene one day. He felt if they did not fight back that the Judeo-Christian dinosaurs and Judeo-Christian species in the future would become targets again and face depopulation programs. Foreign enemies could invade their nation knowing the enemy's stated and written goal is to wipe them out and conquer and steal their Homeland.

Dinodon's comments led Dinomoses and Dinojob to re-examine the situation that looked dim. It appears that we were correct about Obamasaurus and his disdain for the Judeo-Christian nation and dino-citizens. He can't control his deep seeded hate for light to medium skin dinosaurs. He tried to fight it, but his pain over being rejected because of his skin color overtakes him.

It appears that he is insecure because of those who mentored and brainwashed him as a child and messed him up, especially his white mother who left him with his grandparents and a nanny quite often. It appears that those involved in his youth groomed him to come against the Judeo-Christian dino-citizens. Perhaps, this was pre planned and his mentors may have chosen his black-white parents so they could use him for political agendas in the future.

After all, the secret societies have been around since Dino and Dina when the reptilian snake seduced Dina to taste the fruit of God's forbidden Tree of Knowledge that took away her innocence. She seduced Dino and took away his innocence. And the entire goal of the reptilian snake is to conquer God's power.

**The Mad Scientist: Dr. Le Fauccini researching viruses
that could spread to Judeo-Christian dinosaurs.**

Noah decoded another section of the Tablets that revealed more about these sinister agendas. He read that the reptilian dinosaur Scientist, Dr. Le Fauccini, approved using aborted fetuses or late term babies for experiments and that he was researching cloning and creating a superior race that couldn't procreate.

This was another reason that Dinomoses planned the exodus. Fortunately, God appears to have shielded the opening of the cave from anti-Judeo-Christians so they could never find those who joined in the exodus. After all, Noah nearly gave up when he arrived after searching for the cave for quite some time.

Dinomoses etched the following into the Tablet, "I will probably be the last of the Judeo-Christian dinosaurs to die upon the earth. "I have lived a long life and witnessed the greatest Judeo-Christian Dinosaur Nation ever developed in the earth's history. I am sad. My best friend, Dinojob, passed away. Dinodon left the cave and I haven't seen him since. I heard a rumor that Obamasaurus died during the ice age inside his mansion, but I don't know for sure. Perhaps, Dinodon left this cave to figure out if he could restore the Judeo-Christian Dinosaur Nation and if any Judeo-Christian dinosaurs survived. We did freeze the eggs inside the cave.

Noah took a deep breath and he stopped for a few minutes to catch his breath. He felt bonded with Dinomoses and Dinojob and Dinodon. He felt their pain as they tried so hard to save the Judeo-Christian dinosaurs from depopulation and extinction, but perhaps, to no avail or maybe they did as I didn't explore deeper into the cave. And, I didn't think about the frozen eggs crossed his mind.

The magnificent dinosaur, Obamasuarus also known as Dinobari was a force that couldn't be stopped soon enough, but maybe, this was intentional by God and part of his plan for America.

Noah believed that two elderly male dinosaurs who survived for years during the Ice Age and remained in the secret cave were Dinojob and Dinomoses. He wasn't sure what happened to Dinodon or if Obamasaurus was actually killed in his home during the ice age After all, there were rumors by the tribes who lived in the nearby villages that they had seen glimpses of Obamasaurus in this remote area of the jungle. Maybe, that's why they left offerings because they still fear him.

Noah believed that the petrified dinosaur bones that he discovered belonged to male dinosaurs. He realized that the two young dinosaurs had to be conceived by male and female heterosexual dinosaurs, who appear to have joined the exodus, with intent to give birth in a safe place and avoid the abortion mandate, but how many could there be deeper inside the cave, he wondered.

Noah read the last message carved into stone by Dinomoses which read, "To the chosen one, I believe that you shall be of a different species and you shall decode these Tablets after many generations have passed. I predict the name of the chosen one who will decode these Tablets is Noah. This is confirmation that you are the chosen one to deliver the message to your species." Noah was surprised. And, he felt excited to see his name etched in stone.

Noah was excited and saddened by Dinomoses' message.

"Upon your discovery of these dinosaur Tablets, let me state that it was too late for our Judeo-Christian Dinosaur Nation to stop the unidentified reptilian dinosaur, Obamasaurus, from changing and transforming our nation into a foreign nation of anti-Judeo-Christian foreign ideologies. Most of our dino-citizens didn't understand that he came to depopulate our species and overpopulate our nation with foreigners and conquer it, which he did.

Noah found the Message Left Behind by Dinomoses:

"This is the message you must share. Inform your species that they must fight back against evil and never accept "tolerance" and "political correctness" or you will end up wearing facial coverings to silence you and to appease foreign enemies who wear mandated masks coverings as they migrate into your land. Masks are used to silence you and your species forever. Resist. God created Fresh Oxygen – Air – Ventilation needed to breathe into your lungs as the "Breath of Life.""

"And, your species must remain pro-active and prohibit any leader from becoming a dictator and ruling your nation by unconstitutional mandates. Your species must guard their voting rights and fight for integrity and for honest elections. Demand that every candidate be vetted. Transparent. Background checked. Require a Certified vetted Birth Certificate be attached to each application. Secure your borders. Identify and vet every person who approaches your borders.

This is not racism. It is common sense to protect your sovereignty and your species from harm or being made homeless. Preserve your Judeo-Christian laws that include your God-given right to Free Will and Free Choice and "Due Process of Law" or else you will be found guilty until proven innocent and indefinitely detained by mob rule. No one should be indefinitely detained who is not a criminal and especially those who are healthy. The sick isolate themselves at home or in a hospital without the government using anyone as human lab rats and for sinister reasons.

Noah's eyes became watery. He decoded the last P.S.: "Remember, it's never too late to save your nation from depopulation and from extinction. I know that by the time you read these messages that your nation will be at a crossroads. Obviously, I believe that I may be the last Elder male dinosaur to survive. Time is running out for me. It wasn't possible to pro-create any longer because of the mandated abortion of female babies enacted by Obamasaurus.

There were few females of marrying age so we had them join us in this exodus so they would be safe.

He wrote that Obamasaurus replaced heterosexual traditional marriage with same-sex indoctrination of dino-kids from 5 years old to 18 years old as part of his depopulation programs since same-sex couples can't procreate. People can choose freely, but children shouldn't be used and abused. It's child abuse to deny the youth their right to choose by brainwashing them. Kids should never be indoctrinated by adult leaders enticed by incentives offered by wealthy dino-men.

Your nation will be guilty of shedding the blood of God's creation as a depopulation program by the time you read this Tablet. Your nation will be guilty of allowing little kids to be indoctrinated and taught sexual preferences in your schools robbing them of their innocence by the time you read this.

This is immoral and unethical and child abuse. Your species must wash their hands of these sinister agendas. God will not tolerate the shedding of blood as part of the depopulation program. God created procreation so that babies would grow up to love their country and fellow citizens and continue to preserve their sovereign nations. Nations whose birth rates diminish will be overrun by foreigners who overpopulate and will conquer nations and replace Judeo-Christian law and way of life.

Noah smiled and said, "Thanks, you two heroes. Thanks for sharing the secret to awaken our species known as human beings. Our species is working overtime on self-destruction. Thanks, Dinojob. You suffered a lot upon the earth, but you always trusted God. He paused as he stared at the petrified bones of Dinomoses and stated, "Dinomoses, you truly were one of the greatest Leaders upon the earth.

We will remember you and the Judeo-Christian Nation. I hope it's not too late to save our species who is being depopulated through radiation, microwaves, EMP's, chemicals, chemical-laden experimental injections, abortions and famine. People can be depopulated by contaminated water, soil and food.

Noah recalled reading that the scientists can clone animals and people and replace people with robotoids or humanoids. And, recently he recalled reading that children were being confused about their gender ID through the school system and groomed for sex change operations as part of the depopulation program. He felt sad for the children. Kids should not be indoctrinated into same-sex or Trans Humans without parental consent or in Noah's opinion for any reason and changed into cyborgs.

Noah gathered his belongings. He sat down for a moment to gather his thoughts and try to use his photographic memory of all he discovered inside the hidden cave. After all, he was the first human being to discover these wonders of the world. He sat quietly in deep thought when a strong presence startled him. He looked up. Noah was surprised. He stood up. He was thrilled. "Oh my gosh, it's really you, Dr. Lee. I'm so happy to see you. I can't thank you enough for choosing me for this mission," Noah blurted out.

Dr. Lee said, "Noah, you've done a remarkable job. And, you've made a wise choice to leave the secret and rare dinosaur Tablets undisturbed. We are pleased that you didn't give up on your mission. You passed the test. You shall be rewarded in the future. After you return to the university, write the book and do speaking tours. Share the message and save humanity. Your species is on the verge of being made extinct by the New World Order members seeking control and power over your nation and the world. They seek to redistribute the wealth of your Judeo-Christian Nation to themselves and erase all that God created upon the earth including each person's DNA and seek to control each person's brain. They are at war with your Judeo-Christian God. You can now leave your mark in the world."

Noah said, "Thank You, Dr Lee. I shall do as you've instructed. I now understand the urgency of this message for mankind, but will I see you again?" Dr. Lee smiled. He said, "No. Not in this life. You've only just begun, but I shall be watching you from afar. My mission is complete here. I shall leave my walking stick with you as a reminder that I am not far away. I am not a figment of your imagination. I must leave you now so you can prepare for your future mission. We will be watching from afar. Good-bye, my dear friend, Noah." In the blink of an eye, Dr. Lee vanished once again. Noah felt endured to Dr. Lee.

Noah's eyes filled with tears at that moment. He realized that his mission was complete for now. He needed this information in order to share the message left behind by Dinomoses. He was in disbelief that he was chosen to bring the message back to America and hopefully save the greatest Republic ever developed. Noah now understood what Dr. Lee stated when he said that he must complete his mission and fulfill his destiny. In a sad and crackling voice, Noah said, "Good-bye, Dr. Lee. It was my great honor to meet you."

Although, Dr. Lee vanished into thin air, the beautifully crafted Mother of Pearl walking stick designed with precious stones and strange writing was left behind for Noah to treasure for the rest of his days upon the earth. Noah felt honored that Dr. Lee gifted him with his precious walking stick. He whispered, "Thank you, Dr. Lee. I shall cherish this gift always."

Noah stood up and stretched. He grabbed his backpack and slung it over his shoulders. He walked towards the entrance of the secret hidden cave. As he stepped to walk out of the cave, he turned back and took a last look and tried to capture all the marvelous treasures that he discovered.

Noah had painted his name and date on a large piece of wood and secured it next to the dinosaur Tablets. He felt honored to have been chosen for this mission and learned to just accept it and not question it. He breathed in the floral essence of the tropical plants one more time and listened for a moment to the sounds of the melodic water fall and stared at the aura of colors surrounding the stalactites and the rainbow over the pond of water. He slowly turned towards the entrance and walked out of the cave and headed back to America.

This once in a lifetime experience changed Noah's life forever. Noah would never read about the history of the world and take it for granted. He felt blessed and believed he was one of the luckiest human beings on the planet and he was humbled and grateful.

Once he reached camp, he tore down his tent and packed it up. Noah carved his name and the dates of his visit into a sturdy old tree and once he finished, he grabbed his bike and jumped on it. He turned to take one last look at the secret cave inside of the isolated majestic mountain. He rubbed his eyes and smiled with surprise. Noah was shocked. He swore he saw the spirits of Dinomoses and Dinojob, Dinodon, and Dr. Lee waving at him from the majestic mountain top next to the opening of the secret cave. Noah waved back and smiled. He knew that he couldn't tell anyone about everything that he experienced because they would discredit his information, so he would stick to the facts.

Noah grabbed his bike and was turning away from the mountain and as he turned his head to point the bike in the right direction, he suddenly stopped in his tracks. Right before his eyes, he saw Obamasaurus skipping through the trees as Noah climbed on his bike. It was as if Obamasaurus was saying, "Thanks, Noah, for not removing the Tablets." Noah peddled away into the jungles in awe of what he saw. Obamasaurus was the most magnificent dinosaur that God created. It was as if Noah's childhood dream came true in that instant. Noah shouted, "Thank You, Obamasaurus or Dinobari – which ever you prefer." Obamasaurus disappeared into the jungles. Noah hopped on his bike and began peddling towards the village overwhelmed with all that he experienced and hoping to see Solomon in the village and get a ride back to the airport. He had given Solomon the date and time that he would need a ride back to the airport and he was hoping that Solomon remembered to write the date on his schedule.

Noah Catches a Glimpse of Obamasaurus

As Noah peddled closer to the village, he thought, I can't wait to get back home and see my friends again. Sit down with them. Laugh. Drink a cold beer. Chat. Joke. Play Pool. He thought about his neighborhood and his walks home from the university on warm summer nights. He enjoyed the fragrances of the Rose Gardens and Gardenia bushes along the way because they reminded him of his childhood when he and his friends chased Butterflies. Noah thought, about how great it will be to get back to America. He felt more appreciative of his home. He said, "I can't wait to sleep in my own bed again. I never want to sleep on a cot again." His mind wandered. I know I will crash once I hit the mattress and lay my head on my pillow. It really is a great pillow. His mind kept going as he peddled back to the village. He remembered the book he set aside. I should grab the book that I kept setting aside written by Ronald Reagan entitled, "The Conscience of a Nation." Maybe, President Reagan was smarter than the average bear and left his mark behind as a warning to our nation to be aware if America ever approved of eugenics and abortions on demand. He wondered what was it that Presidents Reagan, Kennedy and Eisenhower knew as they each attempted to warn Americans.

Noah was relieved when he peddled into the village. He saw Solomon's rusty old cab and wobbly tires still hanging on. He walked his bike into the tavern and Solomon saw Noah. He jumped up and said,

"Noah, my friend. How are you? Do you need a ride to the airport? Noah nodded umm hmm. Solomon ordered an ice-cold beer for Noah. Noah said, "Thanks Prince Solomon, I needed this. And, yes, I definitely need a ride to the airport."

After they finished their beers, Noah and Solomon packed up the cab. Noah and Solomon felt a bond of friendship between them as if they had been old friends and had a secret that no one else knew. In reality, they did. Sometimes there's a chemistry between people who bond. Solomon asked, "Noah, did you find what you were looking for?"

Noah said, "I not only found everything I set out to discover, but I found more than I could have ever imagined. I'm thrilled."

"Do you think you'll ever be back?" Solomon asked.

"I don't know. I think my mission here is complete and I have more to do in America and I can't wait to get started. I'm going to write a book." he said.

"Well, don't forget me. I would like to read your book," he stated.

"I will sign a copy and send you the first copy, my friend," he replied.

After, they arrived at the airport and said good-bye, it was just a brief wait and Noah was on his way back to America. He slept most of the way back. He was excited when the plane landed in the good old USA. No matter how bad things may seem, it's always great to return to America.

Noah couldn't wait to begin his new mission and share the message that Dinomoses left behind. He got off the plane and walked to the luggage area while thinking, if we don't wake up soon, the Liberals and the deep state billionaires could cause human beings to end up on an endangered species list. Noah grabbed his luggage and waived at the driver. He was holding a sign with Noah's name above his head. They carried the luggage and bike to the uber and packed it up and headed home.

As Noah was looking at everything along the way after being gone for so long, he couldn't believe his eyes. As they neared his neighborhood and turned the corner, he noticed a new restaurant in town. It was named, Dr. Lee's Cave.

The window was lit up with two illuminated chopsticks reminding him of Dr. Lee's unique walking stick. Flashing red letters read, "Welcome to your destiny. Come on in."

Noah was intrigued and questioned the word, "Cavé?" He wondered if that was intentional and another magical message for encouragement from Dr. Lee. Maybe, my mission has only just begun, he thought. After arriving home and carrying the suitcases and bike into the house, his only goal was to jump into his warm cozy bed and get a good night sleep.

In the morning, it was back to his usual routine. He grabbed a cup of coffee and the newspaper off the porch and sat down at the table. Noah read that the new President of the USA declared a pandemic and ordered every American to be jabbed or else be punished. He was ordering every American to allow Big Pharma and investors to use every human being as Human Lab Rats for Big Pharma's experimental and trial genetically engineered injections over a flu or else be punished with huge fines and jail.

Noah was shocked. He said, "I have to do something to help my Judeo-Christian Nation wake up. He said, "History really does repeat itself." Noah opened a letter from the university. He couldn't believe what he was reading. It said that he must get the experimental and trial genetically engineered mRNA injection without choice before returning to work. How is it possible that employers can force employees to be human lab rats without any liability for injury or death?

Noah wondered if the information that he learned in the jungles of Africa inside a secret cave could be the beginning of the end of humanity by altering our God-given DNA as he read in the Sci-fi story. How can they violate constitutional law and Human Rights Law and take every human hostage as their property, chattel, slaves or force any American into servitude to the wealthy investors?

Noah could no longer sit on the sidelines because in the past, he didn't want to rock the boat at the university, where he once had a job. He grabbed his laptop and opened it up and turned it on and googled "Nuremberg Codes" and "Human Rights violations." Noah was about to embark on his next mission and time was of the essence. He wasn't sure if he would succeed, but he believed he must try.

Obamasaurus; Human Rights Violations Imposed by Mandates?

"All Laws Which are Repugnant to the Constitution are null and void." Marbury vs. Madison, 5 U.S. (Cranch) 137, 174, 176 (1803)

A KEEPSAKE and REMINDER

Obamasaurus is a fictional book, political satire and relaunched with the a new twist formerly published as the Irwin award-winning, "Obamacare, Dinosaurs Rednecks & Radicals pub. 2013. This political satire is written to remind free people who believe they were created by God and those who wonder if it's possible that a few evil men and women could conspire to wipe out humanity by 90%? Is it possible that wealthy people who join secret societies conspire to manipulate each person's God-given DNA in order to hookup human bodies and minds to the internet for Bodies, so every survivor will be controlled by AI and turned into mindless zombies who don't procreate or think for themselves? Mindless changed bodies who walk around without any memory of God or America and without emotions. Their minds erased of all emotions such as love, hurt, sorrow, compassion, forgiveness, mercy, confusion, anger, fear, happiness, joy, curiosity, kindness, and so many more feelings that humans experience over a lifetime? How would you feel and what would you do about it if that technology had arrived?

God Bless, Rose M. Colombo

ABOUT THE AUTHOR

Rose Colombo, an award winning published author, writer, poet, cable TV producer and Host featured in international full page magazines, newspapers, as well as her award winning book, "Fight Back Legal Abuse: How to Protect Yourself From Your Own Attorney," recommended by radio and newspapers around the nation. She's won many awards for her contributions such as the Jeannie Angel Award presented by the So. California Motion Picture Council, and the Journalism of Arts, Media Breakfast Club, Poet of Merit, Poet Scholar, and Poet Fellow presented by the prestigious Nobel House, NY and London as well as the International Society of Poets. She's been seen on television and heard on radio as an authority and a crusader fighting back and exposing injustices. Rose was an award-winning licensed Beauty Advisor and travelled around the nation for major skin care and cosmetic lines. She's a long time legal coach and activist. She proposed laws that have been implemented in the state of California. Email: onecupmore@ yahoo.com